Surviving the Jungle

Imelda Megannety

Imelda Megannety
Surviving the Jungle

Song without words
Kaleidoscope
Her Sixth Sense
Return to Moineir
The Last Exit
Kilshee
Travels with Harvey (for children)

For my ten precious grandchildren.

1

Where are we?

Rose heard a quiet moaning and then a subdued sobbing. She had never, ever, felt so uncomfortable and hot. She tried to move her arms which were pinned down. Then she realised that the moaning and sobbing sounds were coming from her. Something heavy lay across her arms and stomach. Slowly she opened her eyes. She could see a patch of blue far, far, above. Was that the sky? Why was it so far away and so small? Were those tall things all around the patch of blue, trees? She moved her eyes downward. That was all she could move.

Mira was on top of her and not stirring. Then a long, drawn-out groan came from behind her, but she was unable to move to see who it was, or what was happening.

'Help me, oh please, someone,' she gasped. She heard a movement behind and suddenly Liam lurched into sight. He appeared wild eyed, and his hair was plastered to his head, perspiration dripping down his face. She was relieved to see her brother, for once.

He was rubbing his head and standing unsteadily on his feet, his eyes were not quite focused. Then he looked down and saw his sister Rose. The body of their cousin Mira lay across her, trapping her. He bent down and pulled Mira gently away from Rose. She did not awaken. Then he unbuckled Rose's seat belt which was still fastened.

'What's happened to us, where are we and where is everyone else?' Rose sat up carefully, rubbing her legs which felt numb.

Liam slumped down on the ground beside her.

'The plane came down, I think. I can only remember lots of bells going off, shouting, and someone shouting to get ready and brace.'

'Yes, I seem to remember that too. The stewardess shouted a lot, 'assume the brace position,' and then it was all just noise and confusion.'

Rose lifted herself slowly to a kneeling position. She leaned over her cousin Mira and started to speak to her. 'Wake up Mira, please WAKE UP.'

Liam lifted Mira's head up a bit and was relieved to see that she was breathing. 'She is alive but unconscious.'

'If we had some water, we could throw it over her and that might wake her up.' Rose got to her feet.

'We will have to try and find some. Come on Rose, let's go and look for the others.'

Rose took a few steps unsteadily, and quickly realised that nothing was broken, and she felt fine, now that the weight was gone from across her body.

She looked around. They were in a wooded place and surrounded by trees and thick vegetation. They both looked all around them but could not see the others.

'Let's go further into those trees and see what's there,' suggested Liam, 'there is a bit of a trail there, I think.'

'We must be careful Liam, we don't want to get lost, everyone must be here and nearby surely, as we were all sitting together.'

As they walked slowly forward, they came across items of clothing and plane seats; cases with their contents strewn all over; shoes, backpacks.

Rose was frightened and shocked and just wanted to lie down and go to sleep and pretend nothing was amiss. They were still on the plane from Perth heading to Thailand and Chiang Mai. They must be, mustn't they? This had to be a nightmare.

Liam started to shout at the top of his voice. He called out the names of his two younger sisters and then the names of his five cousins.

He kept it up for what seemed like a long time and then stopped, listening intently.

Rose also stopped. 'I think I heard Nonie just now.'

'NONIE! NONIE, WHERE ARE YOU? CAN YOU PLEASE SHOUT IF YOU CAN HEAR US?'

There was only silence for a few minutes and then a wailing sound and sobbing. Liam and Rose ran towards the sounds and rounding a bend in the rough trail, they came across Nonie and June, still strapped into their seats. Nonie was bawling, but with relief, at seeing her older sister and brother. June was silent and staring ahead. Rose thought that she was in shock.

'Come on, you two, we must find the others.'

They unbuckled the seat belts and helped the two to their feet. They were decidedly wobbly, and June's legs buckled under her twice before she could walk.

It was another fifteen minutes before they came upon all the others who were in the tail section of the plane with them.

Hughie and Alfie were sound asleep, it seemed; Faith was sitting up hugging her knees and so was Bella. They sat in silence, watching the others approach.

Liam could see they were all in shock and wondered what to do. They had to get back to Mira and make sure she was alright.

Liam and Rose looked around at the debris scattered everywhere. Then they saw it! Above them was the tail section of the plane, completely broken off from the main body of the plane. One side of it had been completely shorn off and the inside was clearly visible. The door at the back of the plane was almost at ground level, the rest, was at an angle, sitting on some vegetation. Nearby were trees which had been broken up with the impact.

Liam and Rose went as near as they could and scanned the inside; there was a jagged tear where the tail section had been attached to the main part of the plane. Most of the seats had been ripped out and there was debris everywhere.

They looked at each other and then stepped away and returned to the others.

Liam assumed command. 'Alright everyone, we are all together now, and must stay together until we come across the rest of the people on the flight. Now, Faith and Bella, wake up the lads, and let's get back to Mira and make sure that she is okay.'

Rose immediately thought about June's diabetes.

'June, do you have your backpack? Have you checked your sugar? Come on, look lively, will you?'

June stared blankly at her sister. 'What are we doing here? Where are we?'

Liam answered her. 'Look, it seems like the plane came down and our section broke off from the main plane.'

Hughie was wide awake now and did not appear at all concerned. 'We are playing 'Survivors', aren't we? I never thought the trip to Tayland would be so exciting.'

His little brother, Alfie, corrected him. 'It's Toyland not Tayland, Hughie.'

'It's Thailand and not Tayland or Toyland,' retorted Faith, who did not know whether to be pleased, relieved or frightened. She just wanted to know there the adults were.

'Let's go back to Mira and decide what to do next, shall we?' Rose was afraid the adults had already found their way back, and were with Mira, who would not know how to find them.

Slowly they all walked back along the rough trail that Liam and Rose had found. It was not long before they were back at the same spot where they had found themselves and left Mira.

She was sitting up, looking dazed and confused and was relieved to find her sister and seven cousins standing in front of her.

'What on earth has happened?' she asked. I was here all alone and didn't know what to do next.'

They all sat down and started to give their opinions about how they came to be sitting in a wooded area that looked suspiciously like a jungle and all alone, when they should be in a plane taking them on the trip of a lifetime to see wonderful animals in their natural environment.

The four oldest cousins then decided on a plan: 'If we are alright, we should start walking and try and find the rest of the plane.' Liam was himself scared of what they might find, but thought the best thing was to keep moving. He did not pretend to be at all frightened and this made the others feel quite confident.

'Yes, we must do that,' Rose agreed.

'We must try and get some provisions and extra clothing and things like that first,' suggested Mira.

'I'm very hungry,' moaned Hughie. 'It's been ages since breakfast.'

'We'll find you food, Hughie, never fear,' said Bella, although she was far from sure about anything.

They all knew this; the flight had left at seven in the morning and that meant they had to be at the airport at six.

Breakfast had been on the plane and shortly after that, their memories became confused.

They thought of their parents, now far away. They had been travelling with Alva, Hughie and Alfie's mum and the other adult was Joey, their big sister who was sitting with her mum, further up the plane.

The flight had only been half full and the cousins had decided to sit way down at the back, where they were all together playing games, swapping seats, and generally feeling very free until the alarm had gone off. They vaguely remembered a stewardess coming hurriedly to them and making them buckle their seat belts before hurrying back up towards the front.

'All right lads, enough dreaming! Let's get going and see what we can salvage from the debris.'

Liam was worried about the food situation and the water too. It was so hot and humid, and they were all red-faced just sitting there, even though the trees hid the sunshine. His watch was not working, and he thought it must have received a knock along the way.

They all got up and started to retrace their steps towards the wreckage, stopping every now and again to pick over the debris and take anything that might be useful.

Eventually they came to the wreckage and Liam told the others to wait as he went to enter the damaged plane piece. It could be a dangerous thing to do; the whole piece of wreckage might collapse on him. He could see blankets in plastic wrapping and although it was hot, he thought they might be useful at night, if they had to stay here overnight. He really did not think *that* was going to happen, but better safe than sorry, he thought.

June spied something shiny in the trees and went to explore. She shouted out in glee when she saw what it was. It was the food trolley and beside it, in a nearby area, the drinks trolley.

'We're saved guys,' she shouted and hurried forward to explore.

They all arrived then and there was great excitement when they discovered a lot of fruit and sandwiches intact in the stainless-steel trolley. The drinks trolley had lots of bottled water and other drinks. They had picked up whatever backpacks they had come across lying on the ground and now they emptied them all out and packed them with as many of these treasures as they could.

Then Bella made a discovery which was to prove very useful to them later. There was a metal box with a red cross on the front. On opening it, she found a well-stocked first aid kit.

Liam looked at it and wondered if it would be too heavy to bring with them. Bella argued in favour of it and offered to put it in another empty backpack. At least it became empty after she took a computer and other gadgets out of it.

They again sat down in the cleared area and had what they would remember as their first lunch in the jungle. Everyone felt much better afterwards.

The four eldest cousins stood silently studying the wreckage, which looked awful; so twisted and skewed it was.

Which direction should they walk in? That was the question in all the cousin's minds, except for Nonie, Hughie and Alfie.

'If only Joey had joined us in the tail section,' Hughie wanted his big sister. 'She would know what to do. But she was too tired and wanted to sleep, she stayed up too late last night.'

'Yes, she would be full of ideas about where we should go from here,' said Bella, who was the oldest of the group of nine. Joey was at university and knew an AWFUL lot of things that they didn't.

'She would guide us by looking at the stars,' Alfie told them. 'She knows all about stars and all that sort of stuff.'

'We won't need stars, we are not going to be here at night, are we?' June did not want to be anywhere near here at night and in the dark.

They all conferred again. Should they walk in the direction of the jagged hole or not? Supposing the tail had been tossed about and the rest of the plane was in the other direction? It was troubling, but they had to decide, and soon. Night came fast in tropical countries as Bella reminded them and she knew; she lived in Australia.

Nobody wanted to spend a night in the dark here, and they all thought that it would not happen. They were bound to find the rest of the plane and the passengers, weren't they?

2

Starting the search

They soon found a continuation of the trail they had been on before. It was narrow and difficult to walk on as there were lots of branches and vines strewn across the path. There were a few mishaps as their feet tripped over these and Alfie who was holding June's hand ended up with a grazed knee.

He started to howl then. 'I want Mum, where is she?'

Hughie, who was beside Nonie, put his arms around his little brother. 'We are just going off to find her, Alfie. Don't worry, you'll see her soon, and Joey too.'

Bella had a look at the graze and then insisted on a plaster for the cut knee. They all stood around as she opened the box again. She found some disinfectant, cotton wool, and some plaster and cleaned the knee and then put the plaster on.

Liam laughed and said, 'anyone would think it was a big cut, it is only a graze, you know.'

Bella looked at him sternly with a frown and said, 'in the tropics you can't take any risks. Cuts can get septic you know or turn gangrenous.'

'What is "gangrenous", Bel?' Hughie was curious and impressed with her knowledge.

'It's where the skin dies when infection sets in,' she explained.

'Yes, and your leg could easily fall off then, or have to be cut off,' said June earnestly. She knew a thing or two also and wanted to demonstrate her medical expertise.

At this, Alfie started to howl loudly, and his face turned a deep purple. Hughie looked shocked.

Liam glared at June. 'Well thank you very much, Miss know-it-all. That's just what we all wanted to hear right now!'

He knelt down beside Alfie, 'she's only joking you know, Alfie, June is always messing about. She loves a good reaction, and you just gave her a great one.'

'No, you will be fine Alfie, that's why I disinfected it. You'll be as right as rain by tomorrow.' Bella comforted the little boy.

June looked abashed and lowered her head. She had not meant to alarm the little boy. But she was right, wasn't she? If you got gangrene, doctors had to amputate your leg or whatever was gone bad.

Mira and Rose hurried them on. 'Come on, it must be mid-afternoon by now and darkness comes at six, Bella said.'

At once it was back to quick walking and little was said as they marched along. Every now and then, Liam would call a halt and they would then scan all around them, looking up as well as down to see if there was any sign of more wreckage.

After hours of nonstop walking, slipping and tripping over vines and branches, Alfie stopped.

'I can't walk any more, June, my feet are sore and I'm tired.'

Hughie agreed. 'I'm too tired as well and it's time for dinner, I think.'

Liam and Mira looked around the area. It was so deeply wooded and dense that they did not know where they could stay. Could they rest a bit and then go on further?

Bella reminded them of the darkness which comes very rapidly in the tropics.

'It would be better if we could find a sheltered place to sleep in, rather than get lost in the woods. Besides, there will probably be wild animals about.'

Faith's ears pricked up. 'Animals? Are you sure? What sort of wild animals?'

Bella was not sure. 'Maybe there are, I don't know, do I? I mean, I haven't been here before, have I?'

Hughie nodded excitedly. 'I'll bet there are lions and leopards about, and big, big, snakes too!'

Nonie was horrified. 'No, they are in the zoo in the park we are going to. Mum said, it's a lovely big park and we can help wash the elephants. There won't be any dangerous animals there.' She looked hopefully around at the others, watching their expressions carefully.

The others were now all looking scared as they realised how vulnerable they were here. Nonie picked up on their scared expressions and wailed loudly.

'Oh, I don't want to be here! I want to be at home with Mum and Dad. Why were we on that silly plane?'

The two brothers started to cry as well, and June looked as if she might start too.

Mira and Rose clapped their hands. 'Stop all this noise, do you want to attract animals?'

'What animals?' Hughie and Alfie gazed around with big, scared eyes.

'They won't bother us if we don't bother them,' instructed Liam, who felt sick with terror at the thought of animals lurking about in the dark.

'We have the blankets from the plane, and we can spread them on the ground. Let's look for a suitable patch of ground.'

He tried to make it all seem normal; he had to pretend he was braver than he felt.

Rose looked around hopefully. Bella frowned and commented that they would need a machete to clear a suitable space.

They sat down on the path and made a meal of the now stale sandwiches from the food trolley and drank plenty of water. The fruit was disappearing fast. What would they have done if they had not found those trollies, thrown intact from the plane? Mira and Rose whispered this worry between themselves, and Bella overheard them.

'I'll bet there are plenty things we could find to eat in the jungle; after all, the birds and animals have to eat too, and they are not all carnivorous either.'

'What does that mean, Bella?' asked Nonie

'Carnivorous means 'meat eating'. Birds and monkeys don't eat meat and lots of other creatures too.'

'If we keep our eyes open, we can watch what the birds eat,' June was suddenly relieved.

It was Hughie who reminded them that they had not seen or heard any birds so far. They all looked at each other and had no answer to that.

'Where are we going to find food tomorrow?' Alfie was getting anxious and so too was June who was diabetic. She had emergency supplies in her special backpack but knew that they would not last for too much longer.

'Stop worrying lads, I'm sure we will come across people soon and then there should be lots of food.' Liam suddenly felt starving and could only think about all the wonderful food they had enjoyed in Perth while on holiday and how he had taken it all for granted.

He led them all off again after they had eaten. Now they must find a sheltered area to make a suitable sleeping place and hopefully, a safe one.

'What about the toilet, Liam? I need a wee,' Alfie looked around anxiously, as though he were going to find a bathroom in the jungle.

Liam laughed. 'Look around you Alfie, lots of woods to use as a toilet, it won't be for long.'

'Suppose a wild animal gets me?'

Liam sighed, 'look Alfie, when you want to go, we will all accompany you and make sure you stay in one piece.'

That caused everyone to laugh out loud. It was a question that they had all pondered as they walked along.

Eventually they had to settle on a narrow path between tall trees. They could only sleep in pairs, side by side. The blankets were spread down on the ground, and they arranged themselves as best they could.

One by one they fell into a fretful sleep, wakening now and again to strange sounds in the surrounding jungle. The older girls comforted the younger ones and soon silence descended again.

It was barely daylight when a loud cacophony of sounds awoke the nine. As they lay on the forest floor, trying to remember where they were, the sounds seemed to be getting louder and they sat up, sleepy-eyed and startled.

Liam jumped up first and headed out of the area they were in and stared around, trying to identify the noise.

When he did, he was amazed and ran back to the others who were getting up slowly.

'Quick, come and see! You'll never guess what's out there! Come on quickly!'

Immediately everyone thought that he had found the rest of the plane and they jumped up and put on their sandals. They had all slept in their clothes so, no dressing was needed.

3

We are not alone

The nine stood in wonder looking upwards. The loud chattering noise was coming from a bunch of about fifteen monkeys. They were swinging from tree to tree and then apparently stripping leaves from branches and stuffing them into their mouths.

They watched in fascination. Then Faith pointed at a nearby tree, and they all looked. They gasped when they thought they were looking at a human baby; it was pinkish-white and so small. Then an arm reached out and grabbed it and they saw the mother monkey bring the baby to her breast.

Nonie turned to the others, her green eyes enormous. 'I don't believe it! She is breast-feeding the baby.'

Bella put her right, 'it's called suckling, Nonie, that's what animals do.'

They watched enthralled. Then as though the mother felt their eyes on her, she looked down and seemed startled to view the nine humans gazing up. In that moment, the little one left her arms and started scrambling down the tree, eventually falling to the ground at their feet.

Nonie was the one to rush up to the baby and hold out her hand. The little monkey grasped her hand and stood up gazing into her face. It seemed to them all, that the baby was smiling at her, it's little head on one side. Then before they could say anything, the mother rushed down the tree and snatched her baby away, climbing back up as fast as she could. Sitting on a high branch, she stared down at the nine, holding her baby very tightly to her chest.

'I bet she thinks we were going to kidnap her child,' mused June.

'She acted just like a human mother, didn't she?' Bella was almost stuttering; she was so amazed at the sight.

Hughie looked at the rest of the monkeys eating nonstop. 'I wish we could eat leaves like that, but I don't suppose we can.'

'They are too high up, Hughie,' said the ever-thoughtful Alfie.

Liam thought that they should start on their search for the missing part of the plane again. They all trekked back and folded the blankets up. They had been very useful in making them comfortable.

June and Nonie let out a screech as they folded theirs. Underneath were several big hairy spiders.

'We could have been bitten to death! Oh, I will never sleep on the ground again.' Faith was horrified.

'I don't ever want to sleep here again,' moaned Alfie. 'There were two yellow eyes looking at me all night.'

'Are you sure, Alfie? You were fast asleep when I first woke to the noise.' Liam smiled at him.

'No, it was in the dark, and the eyes were glowing. I was very frightened and just closed my eyes tightly.'

Hughie nodded his head vigorously. 'I saw them too; I thought my heart would stop. I did the same as Alfie, I shut my eyes and prayed the Angel of God prayer.'

The girls looked in puzzlement at the boys. They did not usually make up stories.

Liam urged them to hurry and start walking. 'We must try and find something to eat; those stale sandwiches and fruit won't last much longer.'

That did it. They started off back on the trail with their backpacks firmly on and Bella with her first aid box on top of her backpack and blanket.

The monkeys were still chattering and making a racket, but they had moved on and were no longer in sight.

The time passed with each child thinking their own thoughts and wondering if they would find the missing plane.

Soon they had to take a rest and finished the rest of the bottled water and soggy sandwiches. Urged on by Mira and Liam, they continued but were now feeling the effects of hunger.

Liam, slightly ahead, turned and shouted to the others, 'the trail is changing, we are going downhill now, keep your eyes open.'

It was true; instead of a level trail, it was now going downhill, and a feeling of excitement gripped the children.

Suddenly the air was full of noise of a different kind; birds, hundreds of them, wheeling about and making a right din. Some were brightly coloured and the children thought they were parrots, Bella thought they were cockatoos.

Then as they reached an area that seemed to have the birds busy, they found a bush or shrub that the birds were diving into, again and again.

June piped up shrilly, 'look at that bush, it's full of fruit and the birds love it. It has to be safe to eat, hasn't it?'

Without waiting for them to respond, she approached the bush and pulled one of the green, round, ball-type fruits from it.

'Be careful June, it might not be safe,' warned Rose.

'Well, I'm gonna try a bit and see.' With that she pressed the soft fruit and juice and seeds flowed down her hand. She put a finger into the juice and tasted it.

The other cousins watched in fear. She turned around and smiled at them.

'It's absolutely delicious. You must try it.'

The birds were twittering angrily as though they thought the intruders were burglars and had no right to be there, eating *their* fruit.

The other eight needed no further coaxing. Each one took a fruit which came off easily. There was silence as they bit into the juicy fruit.

'Wow, this is gorgeous, I've never tasted anything like it.' Liam was impressed.

The girls all nodded their heads and agreed with Liam.

When they had all eaten as much as they could, they picked a lot more and carefully put them in their backpacks.

Walking resumed, but this time with happy, satisfied bellies. They had new energy and were full of interest in getting along to find the missing plane.

It was a long hot walk and perspiration dripped down their faces. After what they believed must be hours of walking, they were feeling very tired.

Now it was Faith who came to a stop.

'I can't go on, my feet are killing me,' she whimpered.

This was so unlike Faith the Fearless, as she was nicknamed, that the others stopped and looked at her in alarm.

She sat down at the side of the track which they only then noticed was a bit wider than previous. She peeled off her sandals and started sobbing softly when she saw her poor feet; there were big blisters on her heels and toes, and they looked very painful.

Bella immediately took charge and brought out the first aid box again.

When Faith saw the disinfectant, she immediately pulled her legs to her chest and sobbed, 'no, no! There's no way you are going to put that stingy stuff on me! No way!'

'There is some Petroleum jelly here that might help, Faith.' Bella held up a tin.

'No, what I need is Vaseline, nothing else.'

'Petroleum jelly *is* Vaseline, you silly!' Bella approached Faith again.

'I SAID NO!' Faith shouted in fear.

Liam stepped forward. 'You have to do what Bella says or we will leave you behind, is that what you want?'

'I DON'T WANT THE PETROL-WHATEVER NEAR ME!'

Now Bella took command. 'SIT STILL FAITH, SHUT UP FAITH, AND SHOW US YOUR FEET!'

Faith was so surprised at Bella shouting at her, that she immediately did what she was told.

Everyone came and surveyed the sore feet and expressed pity for the poor girl.

Bella gently applied the thick mixture to the blisters. It felt better already to Faith.

Bella rooted around again in the box and found a roll of bandage in a pack. She unrolled some and gently wound them around Faith's feet.

'Now take off your t- shirt, girl.'

Faith looked at Bella as though she were mad.

'Your t-shirt, you need some protection now, fast.'

As Faith took off her t-shirt, Bella took the small scissors from the box and cut off the sleeves. She then made 'socks' for Faith's feet.

Now she gently put back on the sandals and opened the strap to the last hole and helped the girl put on her mutilated t-shirt.

'There you are now, at least you should be able to walk a bit more. If we could bathe the feet in diluted disinfectant, it would be better, but we can't, can we?'

Liam gave Faith his hand and helped her back on her feet. She thanked Bella in a subdued voice. She felt ashamed that she had shouted at her.

The walk continued, but as it was downhill now, it seemed easier. The vines and branches no longer littered the path which was also a lot wider. The place was full of birdsong and a lot of rustling in the undergrowth too.

Time passed and there was not much conversation now. The nine were getting tired again and worries about the coming night started to niggle their minds. Would they ever find Alva, Joey and the missing plane?

Liam was also worrying. Surely the plane should have been quite near where the tail part had landed? Supposing they were walking in the opposite direction? What if….? The questions were never-ending.

It was both Rose and Mira that lightened the sombre mood. 'Don't forget there will be search and rescue parties out looking for us, we could meet them any moment.'

They all brightened up at this. In fact, they had never thought of this. Of course! People would be out looking for them! They imagined the large groups of people searching all over the jungle, even sending out helicopters!

They had all heard of search parties being called out in Ireland, when walkers got lost in the mountains, and search parties for people at sea when their boat engines failed. They wouldn't be surprised to come across some soon! Their plane had left from Perth, surely the airport people all knew about the crash by now.

Then came another surprise! Today had been full of them. There before them as they turned a bend in the trail was a beautiful sight; a waterfall cascading down a cliff into a large pool, about ten minutes' walk away. They stopped and stared at the beautiful sight. It looked too good to be true; it was like something out of a movie.

There was no stopping them! They raced towards the pool, Nonie leading the way followed closely by Hughie and Alfie.

The backpacks were hastily pulled off and flung on the ground.

Even Faith forgot her sore feet and taking off the socks and bandages, she joined the others, and went into the water as fast as she could.

Water had never looked as good and if anyone had seen those nine, galloping towards it, they would never have believed that these were survivors of a plane crash and were lost in the jungle.

4

Fun in the forest pool

Nonie was first into the water followed closely by the two young boys. Soon they were all splashing water over each other and laughing shrilly. The water was deliciously cool and a beautiful green colour; so clear that they could see the pebbles on the bottom. They spent a long time, diving and swimming around.

The pool was surrounded by a lot of rocks and was in a good clearing with only a little shrubbery. The sun shone down all day here.

When they were tired, they all trooped out and realised they had no dry clothes to put on. It was June who had a good idea.

'Look, all those rocks are in the sun all day and will be nice and hot. It we spread our shorts and t-shirts over them, they should be dry soon.'

'Good idea,' agreed Bella and then the others. They started to spread the wet clothes out. The rocks were quite hot indeed and Faith said they were hot enough to fry eggs on, if only they had some.

Talking of food made the children hungry again and they looked around hopefully. They could hear monkeys chattering nearby and wondered if they would point them to food.

Liam volunteered to go into the jungle again and the others all searched the nearby areas. Birds again were observed diving into shrubs and Hughie and Alfie found a bush with lots of pink-coloured fruits.

'Look at these Mira and Rose, do you think these are alright to eat.

Bella looked the fruit over, 'they are guavas and are very good to eat.' She had eaten them herself in Australia.

They picked at many as possible and sat down to make a meal of them, eating the skins too, as Bella directed. Then Liam appeared from the jungle holding something heavy.

'Look what I found. Bananas! Lots of them! There were monkeys nearby, that's how I found them.'

'That's great, they should keep us going for quite a long time, I think.' Mira and Rose were relieved.

'Can we drink the water here, do you think?' Rose was so thirsty now and their water bottles were empty.

'No way! It's probably where animals come early morning and evening to drink. Not safe to drink, I'm afraid.' Liam looked a bit worried. They could not afford to get sick.

'I am *really* thirsty now,' complained Alfie, looking wistfully at the pool.

'Let's go over and look at where the waterfall hits those rocks.' Bella thought that it just might be fresh water coming down.

They got to their feet, full for now, from the delicious guavas. Then, bringing the empty water bottles with them, started walking around the edge of the big pool to where the waterfall was.

When they approached the spot which was filled with rocks, the noise of the waterfall was like thunder, and they could hardly hear each other speak.

They waded into the pool again among the rocks at the edge and filled their bottles from the deep area where the water fell and left almost as soon as it fell. It was so icy cold and fresh, and the children did not stop to consider, they drank and drank until their thirst was slaked, then they refilled their bottles.

They stood and stared up at the wondrous sight. They had never been so near a waterfall before. The dense spray coming from it soaked them again.

As their eyes travelled down the fall, they noticed a lot of black holes at the bottom of the cliff.

'Don't they look like caves?' commented Hughie who had explored the caves on a beach in Donegal last year, when on holiday.

Liam was suddenly excited. 'Come on, let's go and explore. A cave would be a super place to sleep tonight, no wild animals, insects or anything dangerous.'

He led the way, to the one nearest them, right underneath the waterfall. It was a huge cavern going so far back that they could not see the end of it.

'Wow, look at the size of this,' exclaimed Mira.

They could see no sign of animal habitation or anything nasty and were impressed.

'Let's explore the others, there might be one that is even better than this,' suggested Rose.

There were six caves in all, different in size but each with an even and sandy floor with rocks at the sides reaching right up to the roof of the cave.

They had a bit of a discussion about which one was best, and number six was decided upon. It was circular and they could see the ending of the cave, it did not go so far back, and there was a homely feel to the place. They felt very safe here.

They went back to the rocks where they had draped their clothes and were delighted to find them all dry. They got into their clothes which were now nice and clean again and grinned at each other. They put their sandals back on and Faith her bandage and 'socks', which she had removed before swimming. Really, things were not SO bad.

They then gathered all their belongings and transferred them to Number Six as they now called it.

They decided to have a look at the banana plant which Liam had found. They picked some more bananas for their backpacks as they knew that tomorrow their walk must begin again. They did not know how many more hours they would spend walking and searching.

The light started to get dimmer and they went into their cave and spread blankets on the floor. The backpacks would again serve as pillows. They lay down and a conversation started. They all wondered whether their mums and dads, now back home had heard about the crashed plane.

'Does our dad know about what happened?' Alfie wanted to know; he always got lonely at night. The others did too but would never confide that to each other. They all wanted to appear strong and brave but inwardly they were all afraid and missed their parents badly.

'Yes, of course, they all do, Alfie,' Liam said confidently. 'Everyone in Ireland will know about it.'

They thought of their parents. All the parents except Alva and her eldest, Joey, had flown back to Ireland. Bella's mum and dad of course were in Australia where they lived. Alva was the only one who did not have to rush back to work after their wonderful Australian holiday. They had seen a special offer of a very reasonably priced flight to Thailand and thought it would finish off the holiday nicely. The plan was to stay five days in Chiang Mai and then return to Perth for a couple of days before returning to Ireland and school.

They continued eating the bananas which Liam had brought. They were filling and not as sweet as the ones in the shops at home.

'There will be so many search parties out there looking for us, they are bound to find us soon.' Bella sounded so sure that everyone believed her.

'I think we should shout more, when we're walking. Someone might hear us, you know?' Hughie was very worried and anxious about his mum and sister, after all, they had been on the plane too. Where was it? Were they alright?

Liam started to remind them of their Australian holiday, trying to distract them from bad thoughts.

'I loved that beach we went to first, the best. What was it called again, Bella?' The others nodded their heads in agreement with Rose.

'That's Cottesloe Beach, quite near where I live, and I too prefer it to all the other beaches.

'Wasn't it exciting, that day the shark alarm went off and we all had to get out of the sea as fast as possible?' Faith thought it was exciting now, but at the time she had been terrified as they all had been.

She was shaking for hours afterwards, even though Finn, Bella's dad had explained that it just meant a shark had been spotted by the patrolling helicopter and was probably miles out at sea and there was really no danger. But the policy there in Perth was, that if, or when the alarm sounded, everyone must get out of the water, just in case.

'I loved the ice cream shop beside it,' said Nonie, remembering the huge choice of flavours the shop offered. 'I would love a salted caramel one, right now.'

'Or a strawberry and lemon one,' sighed Rose.

'No, a peppermint one,' said Faith.

'I would just love some now; I'd settle for any flavour,' moaned June.

'That should be the first thing that we ask for when they find us,' Mira said.

They chatted a bit more but as the light was now gone outside, their eyes grew heavy.

Suddenly there were a huge gust of wind, as they thought, surging in from outside. They all sat up terrified and dozens of winged things passed over their heads.

'Are they bats, Bella?' asked Hughie fearfully.

'I'd say they are more likely to be birds, not bats. After all, bats *leave* their caves at night, to hunt in the dark.'

Liam lay down again. He felt so exhausted and just wanted to sleep. 'If we don't bother them, they won't bother us, lads. Let's sleep.'

One by one they all lay down again and listened to the birds quietly chirping and after a short while, silence descended.

The children were completely relaxed and full of food and water and for the first time, slept deeply.

The sun's golden rays crept gradually into the cave of sleeping children, playing on the ground where they slept, changing them into yellow and orange tinted figures. After some time, they all started to stir and turn.

They would have all remained like this if Hughie had not opened his eyes and looked around him. What he saw then, a few feet away from where they all lay, caused him to open his mouth widely and scream and scream!

Some of the sleeping eight shot upright and looked around to see what was bothering him.

'What on earth is wrong with you Hughie? I was in the middle of a lovely dream.' Mira did not like being woken like this.

Faith put her hands over her ears and turned on her side. She was not ready to wake yet, even if the sun was coming into the cave.

Archie aimed a kick at his brother. 'Why are you having a tantrum, Hughie?

I'm missing Mum and Joey too, you know.'

'Oh! For Pete's sake, Hughie,' moaned Bella rubbing her eyes.

Poor Hughie pointed with a shaking finger at the wall behind them, 'look, look!'

They all turned sleepy-eyed to look and then they all started to scream, even Liam.

5

Snakes alive.

The children were all in a panic. The walls around them were alive with huge snakes crawling up, as though in search of something.

The winged creatures they had heard last night seemed to be all gone now.

Bella and Liam slowly calmed down and spoke softly to the rest of the cousins.

'Gather your backpacks and fold the blankets as quietly and gently as you can and head for outside.'

In about ten seconds, they all stood outside with their belongings stuffed in their packs and some had their sandals on the wrong feet.

They gathered some distance away and spoke quietly about what they had seen and worried about if they were safe outside.

'I think they were after the birds, or their eggs, not us,' said Mira and Rose agreed.

'No. They showed no interest in us at all, did they?' June was fascinated although frightened by such a close encounter.

'Well, I thought I felt something crawl over me during the night,' Hughie said darkly, nodding vigorously.

'Hughie, if you really felt *that* you would have woken up and woken everyone else up too. I felt nothing like that, did anyone else?' Faith looked around at the others.

They all shook their heads. Hughie still insisted, 'well I did!'

'You're still here Hughie, so the snakes were not interested in you. Now lads, we have to start walking as it's nice and early and not too hot.' Liam was anxious to get them all on the trail again.

'Could we just have one last swim to cool us off after that fright?' Nonie begged pleadingly.

Bella looked at Liam and her bright eyes told him that she thought it a good idea.

'Okay lads, but not a long swim like yesterday. This water must flow somewhere, and I suspect there will be a river to be found later in the day.'

They all took off their shorts and t-shirts and ran into the water and wasted no time diving and swimming as much as they could, until Liam called an end to it.

Then it was banana and guava for breakfast and water. Before they left that enchanted place, they refilled their bottles from the waterfall rock pools.

As they walked along the same trail, they discussed the night's adventures. It was agreed that the snakes, although not interested in the sleeping children, were very long indeed and looked very frightening, seen in the daylight.

Alfie and Hughie were more nervous today and Liam was their chosen protector. They would not leave his side for a moment. June felt a bit annoyed. She was used to one of them holding her hand and was missing that.

Nonie kept looking behind her as she walked.

'Why do you keep looking over your shoulder Nonie, do you think the snakes are going to follow us? Faith thought that was very funny. She was not at all tempted to glance behind her.

The jungle closed in on them again and although the path was still sloping gently downwards, they felt more vulnerable here, with the trees and shrubbery pressing in on them. It was dark with all the tall trees; it was still oppressively hot and humid. They felt damp all over, all the time,

'Come on lads, let's run a bit as it's not too hot in here.' Liam set off at a gentle trot and the others followed obediently.

Faith and June soon overtook them and suddenly they all felt free and energetic, jumping up in the air and pretending they were birds.

They noticed a stick hanging from a tree and Faith thought it would make a good walking stick and reached up to pull it down.

Bella saw and started to scream. 'Faith, don't touch that! It's a snake and a bad one I think!'

Faith paused, hand up in the air. She froze! It was indeed a snake. They had all stopped now and stared at the beautiful green but deadly snake. Seeing all the people around, the snake quickly slid away into the jungle.

They were extremely shaken by this.

'How did you know, Bella?' They all wanted to know.

'Because I once read about a similar incident where a child thought it was a stick and luckily her father stopped her reaching for it.'

Alfie was crying again, and Hughie was trying hard not to join him.

'I don't want to be here anymore; I hate this place. Liam take us to Mum soon, I really need to be with her.'

They tried to console the boy as best they could. They all wanted to be home and far away from all this danger.

They did not run again, but walked cautiously, scanning each side of the path as they went.

They had walked all day, only stopping to eat some bananas. Going to the toilet was a nerve-wracking ordeal and they did not dare go into the jungle alone. So, when one needed to go, the others formed a circle around the person and facing away so they could see any danger and that way, they felt a bit safer.

Their legs and feet were beginning to ache when Mira held up her hand and they all stopped.

'What is it, Mira? Not another snake, please,' whispered Nonie.

'I hear the sound of water close by.' She turned to look at them, 'can you hear it?'

Yes! They could, and it seemed quite nearby. They looked in the direction of the welcome sound.

'We'll have to leave the path and go through the trees to reach it, I think,' said Liam.

They all looked at each other. They were not eager to enter the jungle.

Liam asked Bella if she would accompany him to explore. She agreed and the two of them left the others and entered the wooded area.

After some time, they both returned smiling at the others.

'There is a river there and it might lead us to civilisation, if we are brave enough to try it. What do you think?'

They all looked at each other. How could they tell if it was safe or not?

Liam started to explain that where there was a river, there would be, more than likely, human beings. They just might come across a village or something. That might be another way of getting help and alerting search parties as to where they were.

When they heard this reasoning, they were more than anxious to go. Hope again loomed large in their hearts.

'Let's go Liam, the faster the better. We might have to find a place to stay the night.' Rose was worried about the nighttime situation. Was there any place safe for them to sleep?

Liam and Bella led the way, pushing vines and branches out of their way with sticks they had picked up when they first went to explore.

As they walked, the sound of the water intensified, and the children were excited.

Eventually they arrived upon the riverbank and stared at the fast-flowing brown water. It looked deep and swirled along until it disappeared around a bend. They started walking again, along the riverbank.

As the sun started to set, they came across a type of landing area, the sort of place that boats might land and take off from.

Liam and Bella stopped and stared. Both smiling, they turned to the others.

'What did we tell you? Signs of civilisation, guys!'

'I don't see any signs of a silly station here,' complained Alfie, looking around.

'Liam means signs of people; human beings, Alfie,' explained June, who was now holding his hand again.

'Oh, I see! Human beans. I hope we find some soon.' Alfie was cheerful again.

Rose who was going to be a teacher had to correct her little cousin. 'Human BEINGS Alfie, not BEANS. Beans are what you eat.'

'I know that, Rose! You can't eat people!' He glared around at the grinning cousins.

'Unless you're a canningball,' added Hughie.

At that, Rose rolled her eyes and said nothing.

They had not found a place to sleep safely, and night descended so rapidly here.

'Let's explore a bit further on and see if we can find any shelter for the night.' Rose was still worried.

Bella was worried for another reason. Were there crocodiles in the river, and did they use this bank to come ashore? She did not want to scare the others and so, kept silent, praying and hoping there would be no danger from those creatures.

They nine prowled around the area, and it was twilight now and they knew the next few minutes would bring darkness.

Nonie chirped up, 'why don't we make hammocks in the trees, there are lots of low branches we could hang the blankets from.'

Liam and Bella stopped and looked at each other. 'That's a brilliant idea, Nonie. Let's try!'

They hurriedly took out the blankets from the backpacks and went into the wooded area nearest the river. In no time at all, they had managed to drape the blankets over strong branches and used nearby vines to twist around the corners of the blankets to secure them.

They tried out the hammocks. Liam was worried they would not hold. The blankets held and it was not long before they were occupied, the four youngest shared two. The other older ones had a hammock each. They felt happy and comfortable.

Later as they lay waiting for sleep, June told Mira and Faith that the hammocks were almost as good as the ones they had in their garden at home.

'Yeah, I really love our hammocks,' Faith said wistfully.

'I love lying in them on a nice day and reading,' said Mira, sadly thinking of home and all they took for granted.

Thinking of home, started them silently feeling sad again. 'Will we ever get home again?' Nonie voiced everyone's fears.

'Of course, we will,' was the united chorus from the older cousins.

Silence finally descended and the children slept deeply, unaware of the rustlings and scurrying noises that surrounded them.

6

Elephants

Nine sleepy-eyed cousins awoke to the noisy serenade of birds. They raised their heads and looked around them. The hammocks had stayed put all night; there had been no accidents: no one fell out.

They carefully got out of their blanket hammocks and put on their sandals, after checking for hidden spiders, just as Bella had advised them.

Monkeys could be heard chattering in the distance. The air was full of brightly coloured birds and the air was warm without feeling too hot.

Nonie went along by the riverbank as the others got their belongings sorted and packed. The boys ran after Nonie, and they looked around to see if there were any berries or bananas here. The older ones were also searching. Food was scarce again.

The river widened into a big pool just a little way from where they had slept. It had been too dark last night to see it. It looked clearer here and not deep.

Nonie decided she was going to bathe and took off her clothes and put them as usual on a nearby rock. The two boys immediately followed her example. They entered the water and began to have great fun. They just loved the cool water in this sweaty place.

Bella had hoped to find more guavas here, but she was not having any luck. She led the others along a track in the woods and they examined each bush they came to.

Liam then pointed out another track and shortly after, a family of monkeys began to screech loudly and indignantly. They glared at the children as they grabbed vines and swung themselves off the floor of the forest and were immediately lost sight of, in the trees.

'Look, they were eating here, can you see what, Bella?'

There were lots of trees and shrubs here and they could see lots of what looked like fruit.

Liam picked one from the tree nearest him. 'What is it, do you know?'

Bella did not know but was inquisitive. It was a brownish colour with a thick, rough skin.

Rose looked doubtful. 'I don't think we could eat that, Bella.'

'Not as it is, but just wait!' Bella started to peel off the skin and it revealed a white fleshy looking nut-shaped fruit inside.

They looked at each other. Bella took a tiny bite from it and then immediately, recognition dawned on her face.

'It's just like a lychee, it tastes yummy.'

They all started peeling the fruit and all agreed, it must be related to the lychee. They ate lots, the juice running down their chins. Then Liam discovered another fruit they recognised: pineapple, but smaller than what they were used to. There were lots of other unusual fruits, some tasted nice and sweet, some sweet-sour which was not something they liked straight away, but it was food and they needed it to keep up their strength.

They spent a lot of time gathering fruit and filling some of the empty backpacks they had brought in hope, but never would they have believed they would find such treasure.

'There are lots of other fruit trees further on, Liam,' Rose pointed out.

'We had better get back to the younger ones and we can have a proper breakfast before walking on.'

Faith hated that word now, 'walking'. Her feet still bothered her, but Bella put some Petroleum jelly on at night, and it certainly did help.

They started to retrace their steps and headed back to where the backpacks were all in a bundle on the riverbank.

They could not see the younger ones but could certainly hear their happy shrieking.

Smiling at each other they put down the fruit-laden backpacks and headed in the direction of the noise.

Coming around the bend suddenly, they all collided with each other as they beheld the scene in front of them. They could hardly believe their eyes.

There in the river pool, were the three children splashing and cavorting and beside them was a young elephant!

The older cousins were frozen in shock and Liam rubbed his eyes continually.

Nonie was splashing water at the young elephant and then *he* was taking water up in his trunk and hosing her with it. The elephant was playing with them!

Liam and Bella were alarmed and so were Mira and Rose. Faith and June wanted to join in the fun and started taking off their clothes.

'Faith! Don't you dare!' whispered Liam.

'Why not? We can all go in.'

'Have you thought about what might happen if the mother elephant comes or maybe a whole herd of them?'

Faith hesitated. 'Might they attack us?'

'I think so, they would not understand that we mean no harm,' advised Bella. 'Just think about *their* experience with mankind up to now.'

Nonie caught sight of Liam and the others standing on the bank. She beckoned them in.

Liam shook his head and urgently waved for them to come out. The others did too, and their worried looks scared Nonie. Quickly she told the boys to come out now as Liam wanted them. The boys did not want to leave the elephant. Alfie was now beside the young animal, washing his back and Hughie was playing with his trunk.

Liam approached as near as he could without getting his sandals wet.

'Come out now boys, I think the big ones are coming and may be cross with you.'

That was enough for the boys, who scampered out fast. The young elephant stood looking after the departing children and seemed sad to see them go.

Nonie and the boys got dressed, and hurried by the older ones, went back to the landing stage as they thought of it.

The sight of all the fruit made them forget the disappointment of leaving their new friend.

They all dived into the fruit. Liam found a sharp stone and he hacked at the pineapples and managed to break them into pieces. They sucked the juicy fruit and ate as much as they could.

'We must go now, we need to start our walk,' Liam urged them all.

Nobody really was in the mood for walking today. They had walked so much yesterday their legs were still tired. But they all knew that they must.

They walked on past the pool and saw that the elephant was no longer there. They were so intent on walking and keeping an eye on the path incase of snakes, that they came upon the herd of elephant without realising it.

They were shocked. These were HUGE beasts and there were about twelve or more of them. They could see a young one with his mother and wondered if it was their friend.

Just then the young one lifted his head and spied the nine. He lifted his little trunk and trumpeted a soft sound. The other elephants looked towards them and waved their trunks in the air.

The children stood still. Would they charge at them, they wondered? After all, the elephants must regard them as intruders.

'Keep walking slowly lads, don't panic or show fear.' Liam continued forward carefully.

They passed the herd without any problem. The young elephant tried to join them but the mother, stopped him with her trunk. Nonie and the boys could not resist giving the elephant a little wave as they passed. They looked on him as their friend and wished they could have spent longer with him in the pool.

They walked for hours, following the winding river, continually watching for animals.

Now and again, they stopped to scan the area and shout out the names of the young boys' mother and sister. They never heard an answering shout.

The disappointment was too much today. They all felt extremely sad and worried. Where was the plane? It should have been nearer to where they landed surely.

Thoughts of school, and their school friends came surging into their minds. Would they ever see them again? Liam felt that he would never take things for granted again.

They sat down and devoured the remaining fruit and stared dumbly at the river. Fruit was fine and they were thankful for it, but each mind was on the dinners they were used to. They knew their bodies need more than fruit, much more.

Alfie voiced their thoughts; 'I would be very happy if I were a bird or even a monkey. This fruit is good, but boys need a burger now and again, I think.'

'I'm gonna have a double burger and chips as soon as I get home,' said June

'With lashings of tomato sauce,' grinned Faith.

'You don't even like tomato sauce,' said Mira.

'After this, I will like everything,' she smiled.

'Yes, and roast chicken and mash, and even mushy peas,' sighed Hughie.

'Fish and chips,' said Nonie, wistfully.

Just as they about to get to their feet again, the strangest thing happened. It caused them to jump to their feet, shouting and waving.

7

Human contact

There was a boat coming down the river and a man sitting in it, a paddle in his hand, guiding the boat.

On seeing the children on the bank, he nearly upset the boat. He quickly steered the canoe-type boat around and approached the bank where they all stood waving madly.

He stopped the boat and stayed staring at them in disbelief, his mouth open.

'Please can you help us?' shouted Liam to the man.

'We are lost,' shouted Bella and Mira together.

'Our plane crashed,' shouted Rose and Faith.

The man continued to look and said nothing. Then he started paddling away again very fast.

The children could hardly believe it; he was not going to help them! The three youngest started crying noisily.

Bella and Liam looked at one another. They had not expected this.

Rose then spoke thoughtfully, 'he could hardly stop and help, could he, the boat is too small to take us all, and he probably does not understand English anyway.'

'He will come back, I'm sure of it,' said June. 'I bet he'll come back with more people to help.' She was too frightened to think of them being left alone.

'What should we do, Liam? Will we stay where we are, or walk on?' Mira asked softly.

The younger ones were still making a lot of noise, sobbing uncontrollably.

'Oh, let's just take a long rest. My energy levels are gone. I thought that our troubles were over when he appeared.' Liam sank to the ground. It was not often he admitted to tiredness or defeat.

The others sat down and the youngest gradually stopped crying. They dozed a while on the bank, but all came alive and alert again, when the sound of paddling was heard.

They looked down the river and were amazed to see seven canoe-type boats approaching them.

They were all paddled by strange and savage-looking men. Their faces striped with coloured paint and headbands with bird feathers sticking out of them.

They stopped the boats expertly, right beside the nine, who were now standing at the edge of the river.

Holding out their hands to the children, they invited them to step into the boats. The man who had seen them first, gestured Alfie and June to step aboard his boat. Then another man pointed to Hughie and Nonie, to step into his boat. They were carefully distributing the weight between the canoes. The other five cousins got into the remaining boats.

They all got in willingly and smiled at their rescuers who just stared at them.

Then the boats were travelling rapidly down river. It was obvious that there were strong currents here.

After some time, the boats all turned left sharply and the children saw a type of landing stage, like the one they had seen before.

Again, their rescuers offered their hands and helped the cousins to disembark. They were led up a steep path and into a densely wooded area. They walked for about a mile and the younger children were again getting tired. They looked around them as they marched and saw there were many fruit trees here too.

At last, they reached a clearing in the jungle. They were amazed to see about two dozen round huts with grass and branch roofs.

'Wow, a village,' breathed Faith. 'We are saved after all.'

There were people all moving around doing different things and they saw a few women tending fires and thought they could smell food.

The children were standing in a group, feeling a bit awkward and wondering if they could communicate with any of these people.

They were stared at and scrutinised intensely. The girl's long hair especially caused a lot of interest, and the women came to touch and exclaim over it. The boys' hair was also touched and commented on. Maybe the blondness of the boy's hair fascinated them. All in the village were black-haired.

One of the women, who looked older, came and pointed to a pot on the fire and made motions of putting food in her mouth.

The nine nodded their heads vigorously and smiled. The old woman smiled then, showing a mouth devoid of teeth.

The leader, as they thought of him, gestured for them to sit on the ground and spoke to the old woman. The language sounded harsh and seemed like a string of commands rather than a conversation.

Now two more women appeared holding large green leaves in their hands. The old woman spooned some food onto these leaves and the other women served them.

They looked at the food and tried to figure out what it was. Bella the Brave was the first to try it out.

'It's fish of some sort,' she informed the others. 'Tastes aright anyway, don't be afraid.'

'We have to eat no matter what it's like; we must, we have not had protein for ages, and we must get strong again.' Rose looked at them sternly. She could see by the young faces that they did not like the look of what was on the leaves.

They all took up the fish in their hands and started eating. It was a delicate-tasting fish, in a thick type of sauce with some round vegetables. When they had finished all the fish, they then ate the vegetable, which seemed like potato but sweeter and finally they drank the sauce from the leaves. When they had finished, and for the first time since that breakfast on the plane, they felt full and satisfied.

'Thank heavens for food that is not fruit, I really loved the carbohydrate in that potato-like vegetable, not to mention the protein.' June was relieved. She gave herself a bolus of insulin to deal with the carbohydrate.

'Is your emergency kit holding up alright?' Bella was concerned as she did not know a lot about diabetes. She knew there was emergency insulin in the first aid box but had no idea how it worked. She just hoped that she would never have to use it.

'Mum packed a month's supply of medication and all I need for my pump, so I should be okay. We should be found before the month ends, shouldn't we?' She looked around smiling but noted the worried looks on her cousins and siblings faces.

The old woman looked on approvingly and nodded to them in a friendly manner offering them more food, which they had to refuse as they were completely full.

'Does anyone speak English here?' Liam decided it was time to explain how they got here.

The three women looked at each other, then shrugged their shoulders, looking towards the men, or to the leader, as the nine thought of him.

The man came and stood in front of them. He was on the short side, compared with the six oldest youngsters.

He stroked his chin and spoke a long sentence, which was unintelligible to them, gazing up at them with slightly squinty eyes.

Rose had an idea. They would mime what happened to them. They started by pointing to the sky and making bird-like movements; flapping their arms and running around in circles; indicating what they felt the tribal people would understand.

Then Liam make a sketch of the plane crashing, banging his hand together and shouting 'BANG'.

The girls followed this up by shading their eyes and looking upwards and all around them as though searching for something.

They did not know whether they were getting through to the people and they were also feeling tired after all the food.

Nonie was yawning and Alfie had fallen asleep on June's lap.

The old woman said something to the leader, and he nodded. She gestured to the nine to follow her. She walked a short distance and pointed to a small hut on the edge of the 'village'.

They entered and in the gloom of the inside, saw a string of hammocks; there were at least a dozen of them, strung up and fastened to the walls and poles that were arranged on one side in the middle of the hut.

The woman pointed to them and then to the children who quickly understood.

'Yippee! We have a safe place to sleep,' said Hughie and immediately jumped into the nearest hammock. 'This is much better than before; I don't want to sleep in a cave again.'

The others followed him and chatted quietly among themselves.

'If we can get them to understand our situation and help us get in touch with the outside world, our troubles will be over,' said Liam sleepily.

'I didn't see any modern devices, no mobile phones or anything technical really. Did anyone?' Bella asked this and there was no answer. They had all fallen asleep.

Nothing disturbed their sleep and no noise or rustlings of any sort, invaded their hut.

8

New developments.

When the children awoke the next morning, they almost forget where they were. Hearing muffled giggling, they sat up and in the early light could just make out three or four little heads staring at them from the doorway of their hut. The heads disappeared as soon as they got up. They put their sandals on and went outside. It was obvious that the little children were frightened of these strangers.

There was no sign of any of the men and they wondered where they were. The women smiled at them all and offered them some sort of fruit, again served on leaves. The nine happily enjoyed their breakfast.

The women again came and touched the girls' long hair. After a while the younger of the three women beckoned them to follow her and the nine plus three local toddlers got up and started after her.

She led them through a different trail to the one they had arrived on. They walked quietly and quickly, following the mother and her children.

Soon they came to a part of the river which had widened into a pool and the water looked clear and inviting.

Hughie, Alfie and Nonie immediately took off their sandals and clothes and jumped in. Soon they were all in the water, splashing, laughing and washing themselves.

'How I'd love some shampoo and soap,' said Mira.

'That would be heavenly,' agreed Bella.

They spent some time in the water. As they floated lazily, Liam wondered out loud about what their next move should be.

'Perhaps the men have gone to find help,' suggested Rose, 'it's funny that they are all gone, isn't it?'

The morning passed pleasantly, and they all felt fully relaxed and rested after all the walking they had done.

Eventually, Liam suggested that they should now go and enquire how to get help or to find out where exactly they were and how far they were from a town.

Nonie and the two boys did not want to leave the pool. They were having such fun with the other three children. Rose insisted that they should all stay together always, the older ones agreed and the three youngest got out reluctantly, with sulky faces.

They returned to the compound as they thought of it. The men were still absent. Liam tried to ask the women there about the men and where they were.

They made various signs, but they could not understand them. Then the old woman put her hand to her mouth, as though eating, and Faith guessed correctly.

'They are off looking for food, or maybe fishing,' she told them.

'Let's hope they return soon, and we can get some information, we must not stay much longer,' Liam was keen to keep going.

'I wouldn't mind staying a few days here,' said June. 'It's like a holiday after all the hiking we did.'

'Can you imagine what our parents are going through?' Bella reminded them and they all immediately thought of home and how their parents were coping, not knowing where they were.

When the men finally returned some hours later, they were carrying heavy home-made sacks which they carried over to the place where the fire was kept burning and emptied the sacks onto the ground.

The cousins were amazed to see a huge pile of moving things and went closer to investigate. They were insects! So many of them! They looked at the native people to see what they could understand by it.

The happiness on all their faces was unmistakable. The women smiled broadly and clapped their hands.

Immediately the old woman had her immense pot on the flames and started scooping up the insects with both hands and putting them in.

'Oh goodness! Don't tell me they are cooking them to eat!' Mira wrinkled up her nose.

The others looked at each other in horror. Alfie looked as though he were going to vomit.

Only June was the calm one. 'Guys, if it's protein we should not complain. We eat almost raw steak, don't we? Or some of us do.'

Liam turned to her. 'You are mighty brave, June. I don't think I am.'

'We should wait and see, it might not be for dinner at all, there might be another purpose for those insects in a pot.' Bella hoped they were not going to be today's dinner.

Liam went to the 'leader' and tried to engage him in conversation of a kind.

It proved to be much too difficult to communicate anything to this man and Liam felt thoroughly frustrated.

Rose and Mira joined them, and they made signs of walking, with their fingers and pointing to themselves.

If the leader understood them, he did not show it by his facial expressions. He shook his head and pointed to the sky and brought his fingers up and down, moving them like he was playing the piano.

Mira interpreted that as meaning it was going to rain. Rose did not agree with that, as the weather so far, was bright and sunny with no clouds in the sky.

Liam decided enough was enough. He had to make these people understand that they must leave. He confided his plan to the others, and they all left and trooped into the hut they had slept in.

After a few minutes the nine emerged with their backpacks on and smiled and waved to the people and made for the track that led to the river, the one they had come up originally.

Immediately the leader and some other men stepped forward and barred their way.

The leader smiled with his teeth and shook his head. He pointed to the fire and made eating motions. A couple of the women came also and took the children by the arms and led them to the patch of clear ground near the fire.

Gesturing them all to sit down, they smiled continuously at them.

'Oh well, we may as well have dinner before we set off lads, it might be a long time before we have a cooked meal again. Just close your eyes and pretend you're eating a hamburger.' Liam was dreading having to try the insect dinner but felt they did not have a choice.

They sat down in a circle and all the rest of the men joined them, sitting cross-legged. The ones nearest the older girls, leaned over to touch their hair.

Mira and Bella pulled away. They tolerated the women touching their long hair, but they were uncomfortable with the men doing it. Rose was sitting beside Bella and giggled. She was safe and not near the men.

The banana leaves were all brought out again and the 'stew' dished out.

The native people took handfuls of the food and stuffed them into their mouths, with gusto.

'Come on Bella the Brave, you must lead the way, please,' pleaded Liam.

Bella took a deep breath and took a small bit up in her fingers. With the eyes of the eight on her, she put the concoction into her mouth with her eyes closed.

They all watched her expression anxiously. All at once a pleased smile spread over Bella's face.

'Wow! This is good, it tastes nutty and crunchy.'

June was next to try it and she agreed with Bella. 'It really doesn't taste of anything, just think of crisps and peanuts. The potato-type veg also helps.'

Alfie needed coaxing. 'But these are insects, how can we eat them?'

'You eat chicken, don't you?' Faith took the plunge and grabbed a handful and ate with her eyes closed.

'Yes, but chicken is…..' poor Alfie's voice trailed off as his brother began to eat the stuff on his leaf.

Hughie chewed and swallowed and then turned to Alfie. 'It's really nice Alfie, just think of all the nuts you like, and popcorn too.'

The meal was consumed very quickly, and the young people were amazed at how full they felt and satisfied.

Liam turned and said to Bella, 'now I know what the saying means: 'When in Rome, do as the Romans do'.

Then the small round cups of tea appeared. They seemed to be made from something like small coconut shells. It was a bitter brew, but all the men drank it in one gulp and held out their cups for more.

After some time, Liam and Bella told the others it was time to go.

They all rose and clapped their hands as a sign of thanks to the old woman, who smiled broadly at them.

They looked around the area for their backpacks, but they were no longer where they had left them before the meal.

The women now approached the girls and beckoned for them to follow them. They looked at each other, with raised eyebrows. What now, they were all thinking?

They were led into another hut, an obviously female hut with lots of coloured clothes hanging over a screen.

Liam was busy outside trying to get information about other villages in the area. He tried drawing in the sandy soil at their feet. He again drew an airplane which showed the wreckage. He kept looking at their faces to see if they understood. They nodded at him and talked among themselves.

Liam kept pointing at himself and the other boys and Nonie who were playing with the native toddlers.

The leader came and sat down and again pointed to the sky. Liam felt frustrated and annoyed with his efforts to make them understand.

Then the girls all emerged from the hut and the men all began to clap and smile again.

The girls were all now dressed in the coloured lengths of material that the older women wore. Their hair was decorated with feathers, and they had coloured bands circling their foreheads.

They looked as puzzled as Liam and the younger ones.

'What on earth? Where are your old clothes gone?' Liam asked and then gasped as a woman came out of the hut with a bundle in her arms which she immediately threw on the fire.

The flames leapt up at once and consumed the girls' clothing. The girls stood uncertainly around, looking at their old clothes. Well, they thought, they had certainly seen better days and were quite worn out. The humidity of the jungle rotted cotton very quickly.

The peopled were all standing around the girls, obviously admiring them in their new clothing. Again, they tried to touch the girls' hair and seemed puzzled when the girls drew back.

The women spoke to the men, quite sharply, the girls thought. They nodded and withdrew.

Now the light was beginning to go, and Liam knew that they would not be able to leave tonight.

They went to the hut and found the backpacks all there and felt relieved. They felt a bit guilty at being such reluctant guests, but they wanted badly to get on the trail and hopefully meet up with a search party.

They spoke quietly among themselves. The younger ones were quite happy playing with the adorable little toddlers. They had such fun as only young kids can.

Nonie was a bit annoyed that she did not get a new 'dress', as she called it. 'My shorts are all raggedy and just look at my t-shirt. It's supposed to be white!' She looked at the girls. 'Will you ask for a dress like yours for me, please?'

Rose shook her head. 'I'm not sure why we were given these clothes, they are really only lengths of coloured cloth.'

'Nobody asked me if they could burn my shorts!' Faith was annoyed. 'I can't imagine walking in the jungle in this thing.'

Liam laughed out loud. 'I'm only thankful that they did not dress me up like that! I have my old dirty shorts and I'm happy, even if they stink and are ready to disintegrate.'

They agreed that whatever happened they must be on their way tomorrow, early.

'Eat as much as you can at breakfast,' Rose advised them.

'Don't forget to fill your water bottles from that stream they use for drinking,' said Mira.

They threw themselves into their hammocks and soon dozed off.

Their sleep was short, however; the night was now full of noise and light and shouting. The sound of drums and stamping feet on hard ground was enough to wake the dead and the nine cousins were now wide awake, sitting up and asking each other and wondering what was happening?

'Is it morning already?' Alfie rubbed his eyes. The hut was in darkness, but light was coming in from outside.

'No, it's still night, I'm sure,' muttered Liam. 'They are having a party by the sounds of it.'

9

Time to escape

The nine lay still in their hammocks, listening to the din outside. Then there were figures at the door of their hut, beckoning them to come out.

The women's faces were bright and happy in the light of dozens of fire torches attached to the outside of the huts. The firelight threw lots of shadows around and it appeared an eerie place now, so unlike the same area in the sunshine.

The nine were led into the middle of the compound and invited to sit in the big circle of men already there.

There were drums being played by two men and lots of talking and laughter.

Then all suddenly became silent, and the drums stopped as a tall figure came into sight. At first, the children thought it was an animal. As he came nearer, they saw a man, dressed in the skin of a tiger.

Their eyes nearly popped out of their heads.

Then the women approached with a leaf in one hand and stood in front of the five girls, beckoning them to stand up.

They slowly and carefully daubed a thick coloured paste onto the cheeks of the five. The girls were startled by this but were fearful and scared of the silence that surrounded them. No one spoke and the atmosphere was tense. The 'tiger man' stood behind the women, watching and nodding his head in approval of their actions.

Everyone clapped when the women finished, and the puzzled girls were led in front of the 'tiger man', who looked at each girl in turn.

Then he mumbled something that the nine could not understand of course. He took hold of Bella's arm and paraded her around the circle of men. He stopped in front of one of the men and pointed to him and then to Bella. The man smiled and looked around at the others who were all clapping.

This happened to the other four girls, the same ritual of parading around the circle and a man being pointed out. Then they were brought back to sit together with the others.

Now celebrating began in earnest, or so it seemed, to the older of the nine.

Calabashes were passed out and there seemed to be one between three or four men, who immediately began to drink.

The drums started again and soon the men got to their feet and formed a circle around the sitting nine. Their feet made a pounding sound on the clay floor as they circled and chanted. Every now and again they would go back to their calabashes and drink deeply.

The old woman had brought a small calabash to the nine and encouraged them to drink.

Bella was extremely alert and beginning to become alarmed.

'That's alcohol, I'm sure of it, don't touch it, anyone.'

Liam told them to try and look as though they were drinking but not to dare touch it with their lips.

'Might be poison,' observed Hughie

'It's certainly not Guinness,' remarked Faith.

They watched carefully in silence as the dancing again resumed. It seemed to go on for hours and Alfie and Hughie were now asleep. Nonie was leaning up against Rose, her eyes closed.

The noise was getting louder and the six were able to talk freely, after all, they would not be understood.

Bella and Mira had been whispering all evening during this performance and now voiced their fears out loud.

'Liam, Bella and I think that there is some sort of a ceremony going on here that involves us girls.'

Bella moved closer into their circle. 'I think they have picked out men they want us to marry, at least that is what Mira and I think.'

Rose and the others looked horrified, Liam did too.

'I am only twelve and have no intention of marrying anyone, just now!' June was indignant at the idea.

'Well, if they think that they can tell us who to marry, they have picked the wrong girls, I tell you.' Faith scowled around at the dancing men.

All five girls agreed. They were now feeling increasingly nervous.

Liam told them to keep calm. 'I have a plan, girls. We will have to get away tonight, even though it's dark. We don't know for sure what they are planning but it looks suspicious. I don't think they are bad people, just out of touch with our world.'

'Yes, the women are very gentle and kind, but we don't understand them, and they don't understand us.' Faith looked around glumly.

'How will we do it, Liam, do we just sneak away and hope they won't see us? June was trying to figure out how they could do this.

'Don't worry. Look at them now, I think the stuff in the calabash is affecting them all.'

They continued to watch and sure enough, the men gradually stopped dancing and were slumped in the circle again. The drinking had stopped, and they all appeared to be in a deep sleep, including the women. There were bodies all around the compound and then the snoring started.

Liam put his finger on his lips, and they all stood up quietly, the older ones carrying the three sleeping ones in their arms. They made their way over to the hut. The children continued to sleep as they were put down while they gathered what they could and put the backpacks on. Picking up the sleeping children they silently tiptoed past the prostrate bodies and found the original trail.

Their hearts were beating loudly, and they expected to be called back at any moment, but their luck held. They were soon back at the river's edge. Liam pointed to six canoes that were on the bank and nodded at their questioning faces.

'We're only borrowing them, not stealing them,' he said, 'hurry now and get in and head downstream where the current will take us but be careful, please.'

He pushed the canoes out and they all got in. Nonie woke up then and looked as if she was going to wail, but Rose stopped her and whispered that they were going to have an adventure and she must stay silent.

'Oh great! I love adventures,' she whispered back.

The two boys remained fast asleep. Bella had Hughie in her canoe and Liam took Alfie, Nonie was with Rose and the other three had a canoe each. The paddles had been left in the boats, which was lucky for them.

They paddled as fast as possible and with the current helping them, they were soon travelling rapidly down the river, lit by a full moon. It would have been a pleasant trip if they did not feel so desperate.

After a while the river narrowed, and the current did not seem as strong here. Liam was leading and Bella came next. Rose and Mira were at the end of the single line of canoeists.

'Liam, we must be careful, there could be rapids here and even a waterfall, if you hear any sort of noise, shout and we must pull into the bank.'

Liam had not thought of that danger and started to listen very intently from that moment on.

They paddled for what seemed like hours, the moon gradually disappeared, and the sky became lighter on their right-hand side. That meant they were paddling in a northerly direction, Liam realised. That was right, he thought.

They were all exhausted and Bella called out their names now and again and asked if they were alright. The answer was always 'yes'.

Suddenly it was daylight and it had come as quickly as the darkness had fallen at night.

Liam shouted out that they should stop and rest and led the way to a natural kind of landing place. He stopped his canoe and waited for the others to join him.

'What do you think? Should we stop here for a while. We are hours away from the compound and they cannot catch us unless they go on foot.'

Everyone was eager to stop and rest. Their arms were aching from paddling so hard. Hughie and Alfie had woken earlier and were thrilled to be in what they thought of, as a river adventure.

Liam jumped out of his canoe and hauled it up the bank, then helped the others do the same.

They pulled the boats up as high as possible and hid them under some bushes so that they would not be visible to other boaters on the river. They had no idea if they would need to continue their journey by river.

'Come on, we need to explore a bit and find a place we can get some sleep,' Bella said.

They all nodded wearily. Their faces were white with exhaustion. June was sitting on the bank with her head on her knees.

Immediately Rose was concerned about her sister.

'June, is your pump still working and have you checked your blood sugar?'

June was asleep and that caused some panic in Liam and Rose. If her blood sugar dropped too low, she could go into a diabetic coma which could be disastrous in a remote place like this.

June opened her eyes. 'I am SO tired; my arms are aching, and I really want to go home.'

Bella and Rose said they were going to try and find some fruit before they rested and were gone before anyone could say anything.

Liam told the others to take their backpacks and follow him. He helped

June stand up and they walked slowly together into the jungle.

The girls looked anxiously around them. There were many bushes and trees bearing fruit and nuts of some kind, but which were safe to eat?

'Are they guavas, Bella?' asked Rose, who spied some fruit she thought looked familiar.

Bella took one and squeezed it. When the pink juice trickled out, she bravely decided to try it. It was sweetish and tasted like the guava they already had eaten before.

Making a quick decision she nodded, and the girls picked as many as they could. There were the usual banana plants there too although the fruit looked greener than they were used to.

On the ground were shells galore and they looked up to see where these nuts came from.

The tree was high and the lowest branch taller than the girls.

'Here Rose, stand on my back and see if you can reach that low branch. Nuts would be good.'

Rose did as she was told and was soon clambering up the tree to a branch that was laden with nuts.

The two returned down the narrow trail, slipping and sliding on wet and rotten leaves and vines.

They called out Liam's name as they approached the place they had left. There was nobody there now, the other seven were nowhere to be seen.

Panic set in, and they turned towards the jungle again and shouted as loudly as they could. At last, an answering call reached them, and they started walking as fast as they could towards the sound.

The six were lying on the blankets that they had brought, and Liam was scouting around for food too. When he saw the two with the treasure they had gathered, he sighed with relief.

'Wake June up, Liam. Her blood sugar is low after all that paddling.'

June was woken and made to eat the fruit and nuts. She was so sleepy she could hardly function. Rose spoke sharply to her to try and make her more alert.

They all had some nuts which they agreed were very good. They made a pleasant change to all the fruit. Liam and Bella said that they must pack one of the empty backpacks with as many as possible for the next day.

They wondered what the native men thought when they found that the canoes were gone. Would they call the police, and would they be in trouble? How did the police operate here? By boat? How would the men have contacted the police with no telephones? They had to get away, didn't they? What else could they have done?

They spoke softly about all these worries. Their lives had been turned upside down since finding themselves the survivors of a plane crash. Behind all these questions and worries the biggest question remained: where was the remainder of the plane and did all survive, like them?

'I am beginning to wonder if we will ever be found.' June was feeling shaky and upset.

'We will, I'm sure of it,' Liam patted his sister's hand.

'We must stay positive, after all, they must be quite near,' said Rose.

'It's just a matter of time before we meet someone who can help us.' Bella tried to lighten the mood. She felt that tears were close to everyone's eyes.

After a long drink of water, the nine settled down on the blankets and fell asleep almost at once.

10

Tiger in the grass

The chattering of monkeys and the chirping of birds woke the nine. They lay, rested and relaxed and felt the heat of the sun on their bodies. The sun was directly overhead so it must be midday they thought.

June woke full of the joys of life and asked if there were any more nuts. They emptied whatever was left in the backpack from the night before. June was given all the nuts and the rest devoured the fruit.

'We must restock before we head off,' said Liam.

'Walking or paddling?' enquired Faith.

'Can anyone tell me what day of the week it is? It seems like we have been walking for months but that can't be right.' Rose was worried; she could not remember how long they were like this; lost in the jungle.

They all sat and tried to remember. How many days had they been lost?

Nonie pondered the problem, her head on one side. 'Our first sleep was on the ground, remember?'

'Yes, and our second sleep was with the snakes,' reminded Alfie.

'Where was our next sleep?' Nonie asked.

Liam thought a moment, 'it was in the hammocks we made, I think.'

'Yes, it was, and then we were in the compound in our own hut,' said Mira.

'Then there was last night,' Hughie was adding on his fingers.

'That's only five nights. I thought it was much longer than that,' said Faith.

Liam was thinking; they had boarded the plane on Saturday morning and landed in the jungle the same day, so that made it only Wednesday.

'This is good, the search parties will be combing the area, lads, no doubt about it, we should see something happening soon.'

Faith and Mira wanted to know again what happened the other part of the plane and why they had not come across it, or any debris?

That led Bella and Liam to wonder if they were travelling in the right direction. They pondered the question in silence. They were not going to retrace their steps, they just couldn't. They were tired enough as it was.

'Let's explore a bit and see if there are any well-worn trails about, will we?' suggested Rose.

They got up and their bodies felt stiff, especially their arms from all the fast paddling.

They headed into thicker jungle. They could hear the river on their left-hand side.

Bella again led them to the fruit bushes and Liam climbed the tree easily and threw down lots of nuts which the younger ones filled their backpacks with, stopping now and again to remove the shells to eat the meaty nuts inside.

After their bags were full, they went deeper into the jungle looking for a worn track. There were trails but not the sort of paths they walked on before. They were narrow and leafy and sometimes their faces were hit by swinging branches.

Liam scanned the ground for animal droppings. He wondered what type of animals were here. He knew there were monkeys, but were there elephants too? He was worried about coming face to face with them.

He stopped after walking for an hour or so. They discussed about where they might be heading.

'It's still northwards we're going,' Bella said.

'It's so slow going,' complained June.

'My feet are killing me,' moaned Faith.

Bella lowered her precious box from her back and opened it.

'What are you doing? I didn't mean you to….'

Faith was terrified that her cousin would use the stingy disinfectant.

The others looked at her, grinning; 'SIT DOWN FAITH, SHUT UP FAITH AND SHOW US YOUR FEET, FAITH!'

The nine roared with laughter at this and suddenly they were all in good spirits and started to feel hopeful again.

Bella had noticed a disinfectant cream in the box that she had not noticed earlier. She now applied it liberally to Faith's blistered feet, which looked very red and sore. More bandages were cut to cover them and the now ragged 'socks' reapplied.

They set off again, but slowly. Nonie started to sing. She was always singing and had a lovely voice. They walked on, listening to the little girl. Rounding a bend, the singing came to an abrupt halt. There in the woods, partly camouflaged by the coloured bushes and trees, was a tiger!

His eyes watched the nine and he was as still as a statue. He looked massive to the shocked and horrified children.

They huddled together in disbelief and were all shaking.

Liam and Bella spoke softly. 'Stay together guys, in a bunch.'

'Stand together as closely as possible,' urged Liam. 'He might think we are just one big 'thing' and not several things.'

Slowly they closed in tightly to each other, arms around waists.

'Don't look at him, keep your eyes closed,' urged Bella, although why she said this, she did not know.

The nine stood still and as close together as though they were just one big block. They could feel each other trembling and prayed nobody would scream or panic.

Time seemed to stand still, and they did not know how long it was before a nearby rustling and low growling, told them the animal was moving away from them.

'Don't move, anyone, until we're sure he's gone,' whispered Liam. 'I'm going to open one eye to see.'

Minutes later he relaxed and let out a 'phew, that was close.'

'Is the tiger gone?' asked Alfie with a wobble in his voice.

Still speaking softly, Liam told them he was.

They all nervously opened their eyes and slowly looked around. The place where they had seen the tiger was now empty.

'He had the same yellow eyes that I saw before. Remember Hughie? You said you saw them too.'

'Yes, it could have been the same tiger or maybe there are loads of them about.' His whole body shivered, and he looked around nervously.

'Did you see the muscles on him?' Nonie had been scared but fascinated too. The tiger had looked so lovely.

'Liam, he might be near, how can we know?' Rose was terrified as were the others.

They all conferred quietly. Was it safe to continue walking like this when they had the canoes they could use? This was the question they debated.

'We can travel much faster by river, can't we?' June thought it was a no-brainer.

'I agree, but what if those people who own the canoes are now searching for us?'

Liam had visions of them being pursued down the river and of them hitting rapids or going over a waterfall.

They all agreed that they must return to the riverbank and use the boats. It made sense especially after meeting a tiger almost face to face!

Wearily the nine retraced their steps, their eyes continually looking right and left in search of the tiger.

It was over an hour before they reached the riverbank and were much relieved to find the canoes as they had left them earlier that day. It was a long-time past noon now; twilight would soon be upon them, and they needed to get away quickly.

'Everyone, go to the toilet now before we start off,' advised Mira.

They all entered the wooded area again. They were all very nervous incase the tiger were here. But they all needed a visit after the scare, and this was now what they were used to. They were no longer shy in front of each other.

'Oh, I'll never take toilet paper for granted again,' said Faith.

'Just be thankful that there are handfuls of leaves all around,' laughed Liam.

'And water to wash ourselves with,' added June.

Then it was time to get into the canoes with their heavy backpacks, full of nuts and whatever fruit they had managed to pick.

Bella felt that June should go with one of the others; the paddling took too much out of her. They were all a lot weaker through lack of proper food, but June had diabetes and needed minding.

They discussed this and Faith asked if June would travel with her. June was delighted to but asked to share the paddling. The sixth canoe was left behind.

Very soon they were again vigorously paddling down river. It was soothing to glide along the river, and they were not frightened at the thought of being in the dark now.

Soon the river broadened again, and the current got stronger. Liam and Bella took the lead with the two young boys.

Time ceased to exist as they paddled. Nonie sang her songs, and the sun began to dip below the horizon. Night would descend soon. Now and again, Liam or Bella would shout at the following canoes and ask if everyone of alright. A chorus of 'yes' always followed.

They felt they were travelling for miles and thought what a wonderful thing boats were and were grateful that they had borrowed them.

It was nearly night now and they became aware of laughter coming from somewhere in front of them. They stopped paddling for a minute and listened. Yes, it was laughter and conversation, heading their way, but not English, they were disappointed to hear.

Two canoes came into sight, paddled by two men. As they came near the five silent boats, they stopped laughing and stared.

It was still bright enough to see the people and they looked like the native people they had left, and their hearts nearly stopped.

The two men stopped paddling and their faces were a picture of consternation and amazement.

One of the men nearly upended his boat staring, with his mouth open. The other shouted something to the nine but they were not in any mood to stop, and Bella shouted, 'Paddle guys, for your lives! Paddle!'

The five started paddling as if their lives depended on it, leaving the two men gawking after them, open-mouthed.

11

Suffering leeches, what next?

The canoes shot down the river and with the current helping them, they were far away from the other canoes in minutes.

June was looking behind to see if they were followed and was able to shout that all was well. They were alone and those men were not coming after them.

Relieved, they slowed their pace. Their hearts stopped pounding and tranquillity returned.

Now it was night and the moon appeared, casting a silvery reflection on the moving water. It was mesmerising to watch, and soon the three youngest were fast asleep in their separate canoes. The five reduced their speed and quietly listened intently for any sign of a waterfall or anything different in the river sounds.

'Must we spend all night paddling?' Mira was getting stiff again and her arms ached.

'I was just going to say we could try landing at the next good-looking spot,' said Bella.

The night was still and there was no need to shout, they could hear the smallest sound.

The moon was so bright that they could clearly see the banks on either side. One side seemed less wooded and looked like they could land the boats there, and easily make a rapid return to the water, if there was danger.

Bella paddled over to the bank, and they all followed. They sat and silently listened while watching carefully.

Liam jumped out and did a cautious tour of the bank and surrounding area. Bella waited impatiently for his return, nervously thinking about the tiger.

He came back and reported that all seemed well and safe enough to land.

They pulled the boats into the bank. There was a wide sandy area, and they left the boats at the edge of the water.

There were no bushes to camp beside and the six were so tired they just put the blankets on the sandy bank and left the sleeping three in the canoes with a blanket covering them. Bella again hoped there were no crocodiles in this place.

They slept soundly despite some little creature exploring these intruders as they slept.

The next morning, they got up and Liam, Bella and Rose went to see if there was any sign of food there. The nuts were running low, and they hated the sight of the green bananas at this stage. They never wanted to see another banana in their lives, they vowed.

The chattering monkeys led them on, and they discovered a tree with low-hanging fruits. The monkeys were busy eating them and they knew that what was okay for monkeys would surely be okay for them. They watched the monkeys as they peeled the outer skin away with their little teeth before sucking and nibbling the flesh of the fruit.

'Come on, let's get picking,' urged Bella.

On the way back, Rose said she heard water flowing. She went to explore and was amazed to find a little waterfall in a patch of jungle with the usual pool beneath it.

They went over to see, and Bella thought it must flow from a mountain and could be safe to drink. The terrain had changed since they were on the river; on one side, and in the distance, they could see mountains, some very large ones indeed.

'We'll go and get the others and come back and have a quick wash, shall we?' Rose was hot and sweaty and felt filthy in her newly acquired dress.

The nine ate some of the fruit which they all found refreshing but unlike anything they had ever eaten before.

'What would you compare it with?' asked Mira.

'I can't compare it to anything I have ever eaten,' said Faith.

'Something between a guava, a grape and an apple?' Liam did not care; it was food and they needed it.

'Not very sweet, is it? I'd prefer the guavas,' complained Hughie.

They packed their bags with the fruit and put them in the canoes. Then they took the water bottles and headed for the waterfall.

Once again, they all were delighted to be able to bathe. Taking off their clothes carefully, they plunged into the cool water which was not deep at all.

Nonie began splashing the boys and shouting. Liam immediately told her to stop. They did not want to draw attention to themselves, did they?

They got out after twenty minutes of heavenly pleasure as Liam wanted to get going. They stood in the hot sun, flapping their arms to get dry before dressing.

Going as near as possible to the falling water, they filled their bottles after drinking some first. It tasted good and was so clear.

They started walking back, it was about a mile or two from the boats.

Hughie suddenly noticed blood running down his brother's leg and shouted. Then the others saw blood on each of their legs.

Alfie began to howl and so did Nonie. All their legs were covered in blood, and they knew they had been bitten.

'What is it? What's bitten me?' Alfie sobbed.

Liam looked down at their legs and could see brown things moving, lots of brown worm-like things. It made his skin crawl just looking at them.

'I think they are called leeches,' said Bella.

'What are they, are they dangerous?' asked June.

'They are blood suckers,' said Bella.

There were lots of shrieks of anguish from them at that bit of information. Bella and Liam bent down and started flicking off the offending horrors with their fingernails. Their legs were stinging now and itching at the same time.

'It's alright, we'll wash our legs down with diluted disinfectant and that should cure them,' Bella felt confident that it would.

Faith did not complain this time when the stuff was diluted with one of the bottles of water and dabbed on their bites with a cotton ball.

'This is really a terrible place,' said Alfie grimly. 'It's not a safe place for human beans.'

'Human beings don't belong here; this place is for animals and we're trespassing really.' Rose was beginning to accept all the discomfort and inconvenience that was now their everyday life.

'The sooner we're out of here, the better,' Bella said. 'Those men must have come from another village, and we may be very near civilisation.

'They could be friends of the other people and will go and tell them that they saw us in their canoes.' Faith was fearful of meeting those people again.

'They might also be very different people who don't know those others.' June said.

Liam and the others felt that in this remote area, everyone would know everyone and that their presence would certainly be talked about. How many canoes did *they* meet carrying European children?

Gathering their belongings, they moved again into their boats and before long were moving down the river. They scanned the banks as they paddled, hoping that they would see people or meet the search parties.

It was sometime in the afternoon that a new problem arose. Suddenly there were a lot of rocks in the river and the boats were bumping into them.

'Keep near the bank,' shouted Liam, 'it's getting dangerous now.'

They all struggled to leave the middle of the river and manoeuvre their way to the bank edge.

Faith had a mishap when she hit a large rock, head on. She and June were thrown out of the canoe. It was shallow enough to stand in.

'Grab your backpacks,' shouted Rose.

They did not need to be told that. June always had her backpack on and never took it off except to sleep.

They pulled into the bank and watched the canoe head off alone and empty, bouncing off rocks as it went.

'Now what do we do?' asked Faith.

Liam and Bella conferred with the others. They thought the rocks meant there were rapids ahead which meant dangerous waters, and possibly a waterfall. They could not risk it; the youngest three would not stand a chance of surviving a journey like that with no lifejackets.

They landed and pulled the boats up the steep bank and left them in the open.

Now it was back to walking again and that subdued the nine. It was something they had hoped would not happen again.

'Could we not carry the canoes? Maybe the river gets safer further on,' suggested Hughie.

'Nice idea Hughie, but I don't think we are strong enough to carry those, they are quite heavy you know.' Liam helped Alfie put on his backpack.

'Yes, and our backpacks are heavy too,' complained Nonie.

'Well, ours our bigger with the extra water bottles and what about poor Bella with the first aid box plus her backpack?' Mira was getting a bit antsy; she was still tired out from paddling.

'We shouldn't be here at all,' remarked Hughie.

'Listen up everybody, we can't waste our energy and time complaining. It will not make us feel better. Remember, people are looking for us.' Bella was also feeling low but knew that they must do their best to keep their spirits up. Sadness and discontent were catching.

Here there was a good wide trail, and then they were off.

Rose asked Nonie to sing for a while and she did. They loved listening to her voice, and they forgot their woes while she sang.

'We look like those children in that movie where they were hiking over a mountain and they sang, "This Old Man", do you remember?' June had loved that movie although it was very old. They had all watched it on a wet November day with their granny.

Nonie started off singing the song and soon they all joined in, and they found that singing helped them march and they did not notice the time passing.

They were beginning to tell the time from the position of the sun and could see that it was time to choose a sleeping place again.

They scanned the area around them as they slowed down. There was dense shrub on one side and tall trees on the side the river should be.

Alfie and Hughie were now leading and had become very energetic after the singing.

'Look, everybody, look at all the fallen trees!'

Hughie went to explore the area. Indeed, there were a lot of felled trees all lying together.

Hughie and Alfie scrambled on top of them and grinned down at the seven looking up at them.

'We could pretend that these are bunk beds we have to climb up, like my one at home.' Hughie punch the air as he said it.

Rose shouted 'Yay, and we will not have to sleep on the ground!'

They all agreed that this was the best sleeping place ever. Only the older ones thought about the tiger.

The blankets were again brought out.

'These are dirty now,' complained Alfie.

'They will have to get us to where there are better ones.' Rose said, rolling her eyes

'We could always wash them in the river,' offered Nonie.

'They have been used so much in the jungle, that if we tried to wash them, they would fall apart.' Mira laughed at the idea.

They put down their belongings and had a short stroll around the area before the darkness came.

They were happy to climb up on the logs and settle down. There was

Later the moon turned the sleeping nine into silver-tinted, statue-like shapes. They were happily unaware of all the various animals that passed them during the night and paused to smell the air where they slept.

12

Food, glorious food.

They had been marching since they woke at sunrise and now it was midday. Chattering monkeys seemed to be always just ahead of them.

The fruit was gone and the nuts. All that was left were the green bananas. The only reason they were not thrown away was because of necessity. If they could find nothing else, they would have to be eaten.

Talk turned to food and what dinners they were missing most.

'I can't wait to eat spaghetti Bolognese again,' sighed Hughie.

'When I get home, I will make Mum cook chicken Korma for the whole week.' Mira said.

'No, I want fried crispy chicken with roast potatoes,' said Nonie.

Alfie stopped walking, 'do you remember that macaroni we had in Granny's house last year, with broccoli and cauliflower in that gooey cheese sauce?'

'I'd even eat cabbage if I had it now,' moaned Faith.

They all groaned. 'Stop talking about food, please,' it will make us twice as hungry.

June could not be stopped. 'I plan to have a plate-sized steak, for my first meal back.'

More groans followed. 'I'm gonna ask Mum to make lots and lots of sushi.' Faith wanted to wallow in these forbidden thoughts of food.

Silence followed as they all thought of the marvellous food they always had and how they had never really appreciated it.

'I'll never leave left-overs on my plate again,' vowed Nonie.

There was a murmured agreement. Then they came to a tree with hanging fruit and could see a lot of squashed fruit on the ground, as though big feet had walked on the fallen fruit.

'I bet that's edible,' said Rose, 'but it's too high up.'

Liam looked around. The branches were too high up to reach. Then he had an idea.

Looking at the ground he spied some trailing vines. Remembering how the monkeys travelled through the trees, he thought he knew how to reach this fruit or whatever it was.

Taking off his backpack, he took hold of a vine, it was so strong that it held his weight. Then he held it in both hands, took a run and jumped and the vine swung out and he grabbed at a branch nearby. He missed it but the vine brought him near another branch, and he let go the vine and grabbed it. He waved down to the others in triumph. Within minutes the ground below was littered with fruit which he threw down. It was covered in a spiky sort of skin, so was undamaged by the fall.

Then he grabbed another vine and swung close to the tree nearest the eight who were busy picking up the fruit.

Bella had peeled off the skin and inside was a white fleshy fruit, quite big and in segments like an orange. It tasted nothing like an orange but tasted both sweet and tangy.

Liam slid down the vine to join his cousins.

'Well, what's the verdict? Is it nice enough for you fussy, overfed people?' He picked up one and began to peel it.

Everyone was too busy eating to answer his question and within seconds he understood why; this was the best fruit yet, he thought. Juicy but meaty too and very satisfying.

As darkness was nearly upon them, they made tracks back to where they had left the blankets spread on the pile of timber, arranged like a wooden platform.

They climbed up and lay contentedly looking at the starry sky, it was in a tiny space above, hemmed in by the trees.

'Who was it who arranged all these logs, I wonder?' asked Rose.

'I'd say there is a bit of logging going on here,' said Liam dreamily. 'Someone is clearing the area, probably illegally.'

'That's very bad for the environment,' commented Hughie, who really worried about the planet and all the bad things that were going on.

'If it's controlled it's alright, sometimes trees need to be thinned out a bit,' Mira said.

'Well, I bet the people who did this, should not be doing it and are baddies, who don't care about the planet.' Hughie was determined to put his view across.

'Liam, will you show us how to swing like you did on those long thingies?' Alfie thought it had looked very exciting; it was what the monkeys did so well.

'Oh yes please! Can we just have a bit of fun for a change?' Hughie got very agitated by the thought of swinging through the jungle; what a story to tell his friends back home.

'They are called vines, and yes, we'll try it out tomorrow for a while,' agreed Liam. 'Now, everyone please let's go to sleep.'

Next morning after a fruity breakfast, they all gathered where there were lots of vines hanging down. Nearby the monkeys were chattering as usual. Liam gave the first demonstration and they all tried then. It was not as easy as they had thought. There were lots of screeching as bodies fell off and hit the ground. They did not swing high but just held on and swung gently backward and forwards. It was hard going on their arms they realised, but for the first time in a long time, they had fun and played with gleeful abandon.

After a while they became quite expert at it and managed to reach big branches and let go of the vines. They felt like monkeys sitting on the branches. Getting down was easier, they just grabbed the nearest vine and gently swung until they were near the ground and then they either slid or jumped off.

When Liam called a halt and said they must press on they accepted readily, after all, they had to find their way back to civilisation.

They walked on, mostly silent, each one busy with their own thoughts. Rose and Bella stopped on the path ahead and smiled around at them.

'We can hear water again; I think the river is nearby. We may have come further along than the river. It must have wound and looped about a bit.'

It was quite near and the nine went to explore. There it was, not too wide but looking good and flowing fast. They thought with sadness of the canoes left behind.

They stood, considering their position. Liam had an idea. There were platforms of cut timber every few miles and here was one right in front of them. They thought that they were being floated down the river; that was the obvious way to transport them, surely.

Liam wondered if they could make a raft. They sat on some timber and discussed the matter.

Bella thought that the vines would be strong enough to lash some logs together and then they could try and paddle downstream.

Liam had kept the sharp stone he had used for the pineapple days ago and now rooted about in his backpack for it.

They started to look for likely vines and Liam had to again swing up into the trees and cut some at the highest level he could. They would need to be long enough to lash the logs together.

The eight below collected the cut vines and dragged them over to the logs.

The young boys then went to explore a strange looking tree. There was fruit growing on it. They came near and examined the big prickly fruits.

They called to the girls to come and look. Bella said excitedly, 'we have these in Australia, they are called durians and they're a bit stinky.' She picked one carefully, they were thorny looking.

'Ugh, that smell is disgusting,' exclaimed Hughie, holding his nose.

They all came nearer then moved away hurriedly.

Nonie made motions like she was going to vomit.

'It smells like sh...' Hughie didn't get to finish as Bella interrupted him, 'yes it smells bad, but I know about this fruit, it's called the king of fruit, believe it or not; it's supposed to be highly nutritious.'

'I think it a horrible thing and not a fruit at all,' declared Hughie.

Alfie turned to his brother, 'you're always jumping to delusions,' he said scornfully.

'CON-clusions Alfie, not delusions; delusions are like false ideas or beliefs,' instructed the ever-watchful Rose.

'Well, if you think I am going to try and eat that smelly thing, you are jumping to delusions.' Hughie was still holding his nose.

When Liam came over to them, he was keen to see what was inside these queer looking fruits.

Bella the Brave, as usual, was the one to try the flesh inside the thorny skin, but she knew what she was doing; she had tasted it before. She prised it open carefully.

'It's absolutely yummy,' she declared and then they all had a taste.

'Wow! It's like creamy custard.' Nonie was licking her fingers.

'If you can just ignore the smell, it's really good,' urged Bella.

Hughie reluctantly was coaxed into tasting some and had to admit that it was nice.

They pulled a few more down to have there and then and collected more to have later.

'Now, let's try and lash a few of these logs together, will we? It would be great if we could get going before dark.'

Everyone worked hard to roll and pull the logs forward from the platform. They were heavy and long. Would they float and hold the nine? That was the only question that the older ones asked themselves.

They could only use five logs as each vine needed to go around the logs twice for strength.

It took ages to do, and the little ones got tired halfway through.

It was finished at last, and they looked with pride on their handiwork. Liam had made rafts before at home and used them on the nearby river.

He volunteered to try it out on this river. They all helped to pull and push it down to the river's edge.

Taking the long pole, he had made from a long branch, he gently pushed out a little way. He kept away from the centre of the river where the current was. It seemed alright and at least, it did not sink.

He pushed with the pole and brought the raft back to the patiently waiting onlookers, who had been scared when he went out.

They all had branches without their leaves that they could use as paddles of a kind.

The backpacks were put on and they all stepped carefully onto the raft. Bella supervised the places they should occupy. It would not be a good idea to all be on one side.

The three smallest sat in the middle and the older ones were on the outside at regular intervals with their paddles. Bella had a long pole, like Liam and knelt at the back while he was at the front.

The raft slowly took off and it was fine.

'I think we should keep to the side of the river and not go into the middle,' shouted Bella, 'it might go too fast and be hard to control.'

'Okay, everyone, just paddle evenly on your side,' Liam shouted.

They slowly moved along, and it was a lovely change to walking. They were able to observe the scenery on either side and could see monkeys in the trees and lots of birds. They wondered where the tiger had disappeared to, and if there were any more.

The afternoon was nearly finished now, and they knew they would have to land to find a sleeping place, but now they were happy as they had proper transport and could cover a lot more ground than walking.

Once again, they pulled into a flat, landing place where they could drag the raft up a little bit. It was in no danger of drifting away as it was quite heavy, so, having found a wide sandy patch they took off their backpacks and put down the blankets, which by now, could hardly be called blankets. They settled as best they could on the sandy ground. Their ears were alert to every sound and rustle, but eventually their bodies relaxed, and they drifted into sleep.

13

Never smile at a crocodile

Morning came early here. The nine all woke around the same time and lay quietly, listening to the sound of birds and monkeys.

'I'm gonna miss the sound of those monkeys, when I go home,' remarked June sleepily.

'Yeah, it will be strange for a while,' said Faith yawning.

Mira looked in her backpack and the spare one she carried. 'Water is disappearing again; we must try and find some soon.'

'We could have a scout around and see if there is any waterfall or stream. There are a lot of mountains after all.'

They ate some of the durian fruit and a few nuts they had at the bottom of their packs. June checked her blood sugar, and it was a bit high. She gave herself a bolus of insulin. She knew they would have to find civilisation soon; her kit was not geared for life in the jungle.

The older five went in search of fruit and water and left June to mind the other three.

The two boys immediately began to make mud balls, scooping up water from the river and mixing it with clay from the jungle floor.

Here at the river's edge the sun shone brightly down. In the jungle it was darker and always felt humid and damp.

The five brought all the water bottles and went hopefully along an overgrown track, scanning the area for fruit trees as they went. They came to a banana tree and the fruit looked a bit less green than the ones they had before.

Mira took one and ate it. 'This is more like the ones we get at home,' she said.

'We'll pick some on the way back; now we must hope for a waterfall.' Bella listened intently.

'It will be hard to tell, as the river is so near,' Rose looked around carefully.

'Water is what we must find,' Faith said.

'Yeah, this country is so hot, and we sweat so much.'

Liam said that they all stank so badly now, that the durian fruit did not seem so smelly after all.

They noticed the area getting wetter underfoot and felt hopeful that water was near, and so it was.

There were rocks now as well as thick vegetation and they could see water running down the sides of the rocks.

It gathered in a small pool on the ground. They tried to fill the bottles from the running water, not the pool; they did not think the ground would have improved the taste of the water and might be full of bugs and things.

It took a while to fill all the bottles up. They had a good drink first and when they were satisfied, put the bottles in the bags.

Rose and Mira then had a good idea and put their heads under the running water. It felt cool and good on their heads and refreshed them. The others then did the same thing.

'Time to get back and pick some bananas, lads,' said Liam.

'Who knows, maybe today will be the day we meet some people who can help us.' Rose was always optimistic.

On the way back they picked a big bunch of bananas and then found more guavas. They happily marched along now, back to the raft.

June watched the boys and Nonie get muddy and they shouted with joy at their mud-ball throwing game. Soon they were very muddy indeed.

June knew that the rest of the gang would return soon. 'You must get cleaned up before we head back on the raft, come on, you can wash in the river.'

'Oh, must we?' asked Alfie. 'This is such fun, June.'

'I know, but the others will be back soon, and we have to travel an awful lot more I think, so it's wash time.'

Nonie went to the water and got in as far as her knees and had a good bath. June washed the lads, and they were soon recognisable again.

They could hear the voices of the five coming closer and got dressed quickly.

June finished washing herself and had just put her cotton 'thingy', as they called it, back on, when she looked at the boys and Nonie sitting on the sand, and she froze in shock.

Behind them, coming from further up the bank was a crocodile heading in their direction.

She started screaming then.

'Nonie! Alfie and Hughie! Get on the raft immediately, hurry!'

The three looked up in surprise. Then their surprise turned to horror as they saw the crocodile approaching.

Nonie and Hughie ran down and jumped onto the raft. Poor Alfie appeared to freeze, then started to run, but in the wrong direction. He headed towards the jungle to where he could hear Liam laughing.

June shouted and screamed as loudly as she could. The crocodile was now between her and Alfie.

The reptile had his eye on the running figure and turned to follow Alfie. There was a sudden increase in jungle sounds; monkeys were really going mad and there were squawks from the birds too.

Suddenly, from out of nowhere it seemed, something swooped down and grabbed Alfie and swung up into the trees. June, still shouting, retreated to the raft to the other two who were also screaming.

Liam appeared at a trot and then stopped as he saw the enormous creature on the pathway. He backed away and yelled at the others behind him, 'quick, grab a vine and get off the path! Crocodile!'

They did not have to be told twice; they dropped everything. Liam could see the three on the raft and it seemed to him that they were safe there. But where was Alfie?

Having swung themselves up from the forest floor and finding branches above the reptile, they sat shaking and shocked, looking down at the beast. They could see June, Nonie and Hughie, but not Alfie. June had the long pole in her hands, and it seemed to her that it was the only weapon she could defend herself and the other two with.

She looked upwards into the trees to see where Alfie was. Then at last, she saw him. A large monkey had him in her arms and was holding him close to her chest. The poor boy looked shell-shocked and stayed as still as a statue in the animal's arms.

June was shaken but relieved. He had been saved by one of the monkeys. She immediately shouted out as loudly as she could that Alfie was safe up in the trees.

Liam and the others looked around; they could not see any sign of him. Liam shouted to June, and asked her if she was sure? She replied that he was with a monkey, and they nearly all fell off their branches in amazement.

The big reptile stayed around for a bit longer and then headed back up the bank where he had come from. After a while they heard a splash and June saw the ripples in the river and realised he had gone into the river.

She again shouted that the beast was gone, and they could all come down now. There were sounds of branches breaking and swishing noises as the vines were used to get them all down again. They rushed to the raft and got all the backpacks on board. Then they stood looking up at Alfie.

'It's okay, Alfie, it's safe to come down now, he's gone, and we better go too. Can you come down?'

Alfie was seen looking up at the monkey and tapping her arm and pointing down to the ground. The next thing, the animal took a nearby vine, and both went flying through the air. She brought Alfie back and dropped him on the ground beside Liam. She returned straightaway to her lofty abode and joined a troop of her own kind who had observed the whole operation.

Liam helped Alfie to stand up and led him onto the raft.

They had all their belongings on the raft and there was no conversation as they all took their paddles and poles and pushed themselves into the water.

They were so shaken by the incident that they could not speak for some time.

Eventually, Rose and the others questioned the four who had remained behind.

'Were they alright? When had the crocodile appeared? When had the monkey come? Was Alfie feeling alright after his terrible ordeal?

The questions went on and on and they didn't wait for an answer before asking another one.

'Well, I thought it was a dream,' said Alfie smiling, 'I mean, it could not have happened, could it?'

Hughie was dumb up to this point but suddenly came alive. 'Alfie, you were rescued by a monkey, no joke! It's true. I couldn't believe it either.'

Nonie nodded agreement, 'if that monkey had not rescued you, you'd be a crocodile's dinner now.'

Bella and Liam and all the older ones were now very frightened. They had slept on the ground which could not have been very far from the crocodile. How awful!

'That's it, lads, we are not sleeping in the jungle again,' Liam declared.

'But where can we sleep if we need to? We can't stay on the river, can we?' Mira was scared at the idea of crocodiles swimming nearby.

'Who's good at praying, lads? Hughie, get on to our guardian angels now, please.'

They were getting tired from all the paddling and could see no end in sight to their problems.

Bella at this stage was convinced that they had been travelling in the wrong direction all along, so were Liam and Rose. They had seen no trace of a plane or debris anywhere. The tail had obviously spun around and faced the opposite way to the rest of the wreckage. How would anyone find them?

This was their worst day ever. They tried to keep positive, convincing each other that people were looking for them. Individually though, they were sure the search parties were looking in the wrong place.

Hours passed. Nonie sang now and again and even singing 'This Old Man', did not make the others feel better. Gradually, her singing faded away.

It was much later, and the sun was getting cooler, when something made them emerge from the sad, and hopeless thoughts they each had.

Hughie started pointing at the water around them. They were horrified to see lots of crocodile eyes peering at them just above the water.

Nonie started to wail then and panic set in. These were big creatures who could easily upset their fragile raft and then they would be eaten.

They tried shouting at the beasts, but nothing happened. They paddled faster and more desperately. The huge reptiles followed them easily and without effort. The river was *their* kingdom, and they had all the time in the world.

The raft swung wildly from side to side; they were losing control of it. The stricken children clung to their paddles and tried to move away towards the bank but soon saw that the eyes were now all around them, completely encircling them.

Was this to be the end of them all?

14

People, wonderful people!

Suddenly there was a lot of noise all around them and they looked to see where it was coming from. There were lots of canoes all approaching them!

The men in the canoes started beating the surface of the water violently with paddles. It made an awful noise and the nine did not know what was happening or why.

Several minutes later they understood; the crocodiles had all disappeared and those scary eyes were gone.

Now the men surrounded the raft and pointed to the bank. Liam understood that they were being told to head there. Two canoes were in front leading the way and the others came on each side and behind them.

The nine were too shocked to be surprised and followed the men silently.

Now the river divided, and a side channel was the one the leader was heading for.

After some more paddling, their arms aching terribly, a landing area came into view.

It was with relief that Liam and the others landed the raft. The men were helping them all off and then pulled the raft up a beach-type area and set it down under some trees.

Women and children now rushed out to see these strange looking white people, who looked wild and ragged and smelled badly too.

The small children were the first to approach the nine, smiling and curious.

The men were examining the raft and then looking at the nine. Liam could almost hear the questions and he nodded his head and pointed to himself, smiling.

The men's faces showed amazement and they kept looking at Liam and then at the raft and pointing to both.

Bella and the girls understood exactly what was being said without words.

'Hey, we helped too you know,' Bella said indignantly.

'Our hands were nearly raw with all that lashing, don't pretend you did it all yourself, Liam,' Rose said crossly.

'Yeah, without us, we would still be back there,' agreed Mira and Faith and the others agreed with her.

Liam had the grace to blush and immediately pointed to the others and then at the raft.

Bella stepped forward and pointed to all of them and Liam. The men all nodded and smiled at them. They pointed to the raft and said a long sentence which they of course could not understand but they knew that they were being complimented on their work.

Liam was responsible for the intricate way they had lashed the logs together. When he was younger, he had watched his granny darning a sock belonging to his grandfather and was mesmerised at how tight the weave had been, as she drew the thread under one strand of wool and then over the next, repeating the movement until the hole was filled with a tight filling that was as good as the rest of the sock. So that's what he had done with the vines, which had taken so long and hurt their hands so much. Then when that was done, they had to lash the whole thing again twice with each vine until it held solidly.

Liam was now standing with the men showing how it was done and they looked full of admiration.

The women again came and touched the girl's hair, and the children were fascinated by the sandals and blond hair of the boys.

They were led into a village compound which was much bigger than the earlier one. It seemed more organised too.

A tall man came out of one of the huts and invited the nine to sit down around the usual fire.

He then called a young girl out to meet them, it seemed to the nine that she was his daughter.

He prodded her to move closer to them. She seemed a bit shy and held her head down until she got another poke from her father.

'Hell-lo! My name is Tato, and I am nine years.'

She continued to look embarrassed and then Rose led the rest of them in applause. They clapped happily and smiled at Tato.

Bella stood up and introduced the gang to Tato who repeated the names uncertainly after her.

Rose had an idea. 'Do you go to school Tato?'

Tato frowned, and then understanding dawned in her eyes.

'Sch-oool, yes Tato go.'

They clapped again and so did the women standing around.

Liam then grabbed the opportunity to try to make the people understand who they were and what had happened to them.

'Tato, do you have a pencil and paper?' He made writing actions to help the girl.

She understood and rushed back into the hut and returned with a copybook and a pencil.

Now everyone crowded around as Liam took the precious items and sitting on the ground he drew a plane, then a broken plane then the nine children in single file as though walking.

Tato's father took the copybook, and it was passed around the circle.

Horror showed on all the faces and their story was understood; they knew this for certain, when an older woman came forward and shaking her head, she patted them all on the back.

Everyone was talking at once and looking very concerned at the survivors.

Faith asked Tato if they had food to eat as they were starving and only eaten fruit for days.

They were hurriedly brought into a big hut and sat down on a grass mat on the floor. Shortly there followed a delicious dinner of freshly cooked fish and some sort of fried vegetable cakes.

The nine did not need an invitation to start eating; they ate non-stop for some time and at last, sighed and leaned back against the walls of the hut.

Tato looked at them and asked if the food was 'goody'; they looked at her smiling and all said as one, 'Tato, it was VERY goody.'

Now it was dark outside, and they knew they would be safe here. The younger ones were already curled up asleep on the rug.

Tato's father and three other men came into the hut. They spoke to Tato who nodded.

'You sleep now, here. Tomorrow we go talk to PaPa M'fee,' she smiled at them.

'Who is PaPa M'fee, Tato?' Liam and the girls looked at one another. Was this the chief of their clan, and would he try to marry off the girls like what happened before?

Tato saw the worried looks they all shared.

'PaPa M'fee very good man. He speak da Engleesh and will help.'

They all thought that if he could speak English, it would help a great deal and perhaps now, they could hope to be rescued soon.

They were brought outside to an area where there were latrines dug and a screen around them. It was primitive, but after what they had experienced in the jungle, it was luxurious.

They were given basins of water and were able to wash themselves a little.

Bed had never been so welcome, and they joined the three sleeping youngsters and were soon fast asleep. A net screen put over the hut entrance, ensured that there were no insect bites tonight.

They awoke next day to the sound of women chatting and children shouting and laughing. On going outside, they saw a football match going on beyond the huts on a clay pitch.

Tato was waiting outside their hut and got up quickly when she saw that they were awake.

Smiling, she led them to a spot near the women and sat them down. They were served breakfast of some kind; fruit and a type of grain bread which tasted very good.

There was no sign of the men and Rose and Mira asked Tato where her father was. She pointed to the river and made stabbing signs with her right arm. 'Food, they catch de food,' she smiled.

They were all rested and relaxed and some of them wandered over to watch the football. The 'ball' was a round hard object, and they suspected it was a fruit of some sort.

Then the boys saw Liam and beckoned for him to join them. He happily ran in and started kicking the 'ball'.

The girls watched and were amazed to see how agile those boys were, playing brilliant football, barefoot.

When the boys went to rest, the girls went and started kicking the ball and soon some other girls joined in, including Tato. Nonie was the fastest one on the pitch and started scoring goals non-stop. Soon the boys took an interest and seemed very impressed with their skill. The local girls were so busy laughing and looking embarrassed that Rose thought they did not usually play football.

She was right. Some older boys did not look as though they were happy about the girls playing and frowned a lot.

Liam noticed and waved at the boys to come and join in too. When they saw Liam join the girls, they gradually came onto the pitch and before long the place rang with shouts and laughter.

Some hours passed before the men returned with nets full of fish. Some were big fish and some small. The women expertly gutted and cleaned them and the guts were brought over to a few dogs that were obviously kept as watchdogs.

Tato's father appeared then and with Tato's help told the nine that tomorrow they would go to PaPa M'fee and talk with him.

They were so relieved they did not mind waiting another day.

Later all the girls went to the river with Tato and her friends and siblings. They all bathed and had great fun splashing and washing themselves. They were given small wads of what looked like, the outside of coconuts, to wash themselves with; quite hairy and scratchy. They emerged from the river and felt much cleaner than they had in days.

When the girls went back to the compound, the boys then left, and they also came back clean and happy looking.

Dinner that night was the freshly caught fish, in a spicy sauce this time and as delicious as last night.

Tato brought over her copy book and an English reading book to the girls, when dinner was finished.

She pointed to words which Rose and Mira pronounced for her. Explanations were funny, there was a lot of miming going on. June was good at miming things and her expressions had everyone laughing.

There was a nursery rhythm on one page that had Tato puzzled. It was Jack and Jill.

That took some miming! June pulled Liam to his feet and pointed at the word and then at Liam, saying 'Jack', then took hold of Faith and again pointed at the word for 'Jill' and then at Faith.

Picking up a nearby bucker she mimed going to the river and pulling up the bucket full of water. Each thing she did, Rose was pointing to the word on the page, so Tato knew exactly what they were doing.

When it came to Jack 'falling down', everyone was hysterical and tears ran down the older women's faces; when Jill came 'tumbling after', there were hoots of laughter and some nasal eruptions. The young children were lying on the ground laughing. Tato kept up a running commentary explaining in her own language everything that was happening.

By the time Jack got up and limped to his hut, they understood exactly. Now Bella appeared as the cross mother, shaking her finger at poor Jill and sending her off to bed.

Tato was no longer the shy girl they had first met. She was confident and the children all flocked to look at her reading book.

Mira smiled at them all. It was a long time since they had such fun and laughed so much.

'Tato, you much teach the little ones to read and understand English too,' she said.

Tato nodded and said, 'yes, that is what my father tell me, and PaPa M'fee also.'

Then it was time for their second night in the hut and they went off happily, wondering what tomorrow would bring.

'That was great fun, wasn't it?' June really like these people.

'Yes, I feel very safe here. It's a lot different to the last tribe we met. Not that they were bad, just hard to understand.' Bella looked at the others for confirmation.

Alfie looked mournfully at her, 'yes, it's nice here, but I want to be home with Mum. I'm afraid that she will have forgotten me by now.' He sobbed softly.

'Oh never, Alfie,' Bella said firmly and took him into her arms for a cuddle. And that's how he fell asleep, with his thumb in his mouth and Bella's arms wrapped around him.

15

PaPa M'fee

Everyone gathered at the river's edge after breakfast. There were canoes all lined up and in each, a man was waiting. One person would accompany the one paddling and they were all relieved that they did not have to paddle. It was tiring work and their arms were still stiff and sore, after all the hours they had paddled.

Everyone came and waved them off and Tato looked sad at her newly found friends' departure. The past couple of days had been fun and the older boys had been very accepting of the girls playing football. She hoped they could continue to play when these white people went away.

The nine waved to the people on the bank until they were out of sight. They were now on the main river again, having left the narrow channel.

They watched apprehensively for crocodiles and hoped they were nowhere nearby.

The jungle continued to border the river and the scenery was all the exact same, as far as the cousins were concerned.

The hot sun shone down on them and rivulets of sweat trickled down their backs and tickled them.

Their water bottles were quickly empty, and they hoped they would soon be able to refill them. The native men were paddling at an even and rhythmical stroke, not fast and not slow. They occasionally shouted at each other; now and again there was laughter in answer and the cousins wondered what it was they were saying.

The journey seemed to go on for ever and the curiosity they had started out with gradually left them, as the hours went by.

It must have been mid-afternoon when another shout from one of the men roused them and they looked around, alert again and curious.

The jungle had thinned out and now on both sides of the river were seen signs of civilisation.

Lots of canoes were around, at the water's edge and men were unloading what looked like fish, but also there were big bundles of goods being taken off the bigger canoes and men were taking them on their shoulders up the banks.

Now the paddlers were pulling into a landing area on the opposite side of the river to the unloading canoes.

The excitement began to grow as the men stopped the canoes and helped the hot travelers to alight onto dry land.

Then a long march followed, and the cousins were dismayed; they thought they had arrived, but no, it seemed they had to journey onwards.

Another hour passed and Hughie and Alfie were beginning to wilt with June struggling behind them and Liam decided to slow the men down.

He ran ahead and stopped one man. Pointing to the others and to the sun, he tried to explain that they were tired and hot.

The man smiled and nodded and seemed to understand but pointed to the sun and then made a motion of putting his hands together and covering his eyes with them.

Bella came up and asked what was happening. Liam explained and they both looked at the friendly face of the man.

Then Mira came up and saw what the man was doing. 'I think he is covering his eyes to show that he can't see.'

'I think it means it's dark and therefore he can't see.' Rose added.

Liam frowned and then saw what the man meant. They had to keep walking otherwise it would be night and they wouldn't be able to see where they were going.

'Hell's bells! How far do we have to walk? My feet are already in bits,' Faith was beginning to fade.

After the good night's sleep they had, they were now all ready for bed again, and the sun was still shining, although beginning to sink in the west.

The paddlers had a chat and nodded to each other. Then the youngest three had a pleasant surprise; they were hoisted up onto the muscular shoulders of their paddlers.

This made them all laugh, and they took to the trail again a little happier.

'Sing a song Nonie,' ordered Rose.

Nonie immediately launched into "This Old Man" and everyone marched with more energy.

The singing had faded away and the moon was beginning to peep through the trees. They all stumbled on, no longer thinking of very much at all. It was as if they were robots or zombies.

Then suddenly there were torches blazing and fires sending up lots of smoke and better still, human voices and children's laughter.

'I don't believe it,' whispered June.

'Neither do I, but it's real,' said Faith.

There was a village coming into view with lots of people bustling about, huts galore and some very long huts, which they had not seen before. Somewhere there was a choir singing, it sounded beautiful to the nine.

'Are we in heaven?' Hughie had been asleep and now woke with a start. 'I hear angels singing!'

The men reached the long hut and let the three riding on their shoulders down gently.

They were led into the hut and were amazed to see so many people. There were rough wooden tables about the place and long benches on either side of them.

The nine gratefully sank down on the benches as the men went to an area that looked like a kitchen of sorts and began to speak to the women there, pointing back to the children as he did.

Soon, bowls of steaming food were served to the newcomers; the usual fish of course, which was the main protein here, but then fruit and they were delighted to see mangoes. Lastly cups of milk were brought out and the cousins looked at one another. Milk! This meant cows, didn't it? Civilisation at last!

Satisfied at last, they all started to chat again. Nobody came to feel their hair and all the people around seemed friendly and welcoming.

'I just hope that this PaPa M'fee is not the boss man and that he won't think he can marry us off,' said Faith in a quiet voice.

'We are completely in their control, we don't even know where we are,' worried Rose.

'Where would we run to now, if we have to escape? We have no idea where the trail is or which direction to head for.' Mira was worried too.

Bella soothed them. 'Do you not remember what Tato said? He's a good man, she said.'

They felt a bit comforted by this but wondered how long they would have to wait to meet this big chief.

Suddenly there was a big commotion from outside the long hut. Voices were raised and they sounded excited too.

The paddlers got up and left their table where they had eaten and chatted together. They went outside and the children sat wide-eyed looking at them depart.

What was happening? What were they supposed to do now?

The loud voices came nearer. There was much laughter and clapping of hands. The women were as noisy as the men. Then the voices reached the hut and the children looked at the entrance and saw a big crowd of people looking in at them.

A tall man in local dress walked towards the nine as the other people stood outside the hut, looking in.

As the man got nearer, the nine looked at him with their mouths open.

He had a white beard that came below his chest and in the poor light, it looked like his face was polished and shiny with bronzed cheeks.

'Looks like Santa Clause,' muttered Alfie.

The man stood in front of the nine and he looked as amazed as they did.

'Holy God and His blessed angels! What have we got here, at all, at all?'

There was no denying the Irish brogue.

He turned around and shouted out something to the people at the entrance.

Straightaway, a woman advanced with a big blazing torch, which she attached to the wall behind the nine

Now they could all see each other clearly. He was an old white man, very tanned, and smiling broadly.

The nine were still silent. This was all so weird, and they thought they were all dreaming.

The man sat down beside Liam and smiled around at them.

'I'm Father Murphy and pleased to see you all. I would just love to know who you are and what you're doing in this place.'

His Irish accent was so obvious that they all started explaining together in excited voices.

'Ah now lads, you'll have to speak slower and maybe just one at a time, I'm not as young as I used to be, y'know.'

Liam started, 'we were on a plane, and it crashed.'

'We are the survivors but can't find the others,' said Bella.

'Yes, and our piece of the plane broke off,' said Rose.

'We've been searching for the rest of the plane,' added Mira.

'And we haven't found any sign of it,' put in Faith.

'And I need to find help soon, 'cos I'm diabetic and running out of medication,' added June in a loud voice.

'We have had lots of adventures too,' said Nonie brightly.

'My brother nearly got eaten by a crocodile,' said Hughie grimly.

Alfie nodded, 'I just want to find my Mum and sister.'

Liam spread his hands, 'we have no idea whether we are walking in the right direction and need some help. There must be search parties out looking for us.'

'Well, well! You poor people, you have had an awful experience and I'm sure many people are searching for you. We will contact the police immediately and you will be soon reunited with your families.'

They all looked around at each other. This was what they wanted to hear.

'Where are we Father Murphy? Is this near Chiang Mai, where the plane was headed?'

'Ah lads, I'm afraid you have been headed in the opposite direction, but never worry now, it'll soon be sorted.'

'How are you here, and why did Tato call you PaPa M'fee?' Hughie was very puzzled by all of this.

'That's the way the people here pronounce my name. I've been here over thirty-five years. We've been busy starting schools and clinics and although

I only came out for five years, here I am, much older and wiser.' He beamed at them.

'You look very old,' said Alfie. 'I thought you must be Santa Claus with that white beard.'

'Oh, I am as old as Methuselah, at least I feel that. You know who Methuselah was, do you?'

They all shook their heads, puzzled.

'Sure, wasn't he the oldest man mentioned in the Bible? He lived for nine hundred and sixty-nine years, so he did.'

Hughie shook his head, 'that's not possible, nobody lives that long.'

'In biblical times, most people lived to be very old,' explained Father Murphy.

Liam looked at the kindly face, 'maybe in biblical times their year was different and not twelve months, like ours.'

Father Murphy looked at Liam, eyes twinkling, 'we have a shrewd boyo here, I'm thinking. Would you have Kerry blood in you, by any chance?'

The four Barber children laughed delightedly.

'Our dad is a Kerryman,' they all said together.

'Well, I never! 'Tis a Kerryman you are talking to now, y'know. We are a tribe like no other, let me tell you.'

There was much banter and joking after this and the nine were so relieved to find someone they could talk to. They felt their worries fall away and optimism returned.

They had good fun chattering away to this kind man, and almost forgot where they were. Being with him, they did not feel lost and all alone.

Then they relayed their previous experience in the first village and how they thought the girls were going to married off to these strangers.

Father Murphy listened in silence and nodded now and again.

'It must have been an awful experience for you all. There are some minor tribes that are slowly becoming extinct, they want to increase their numbers. They are not really accepted by the main tribes; their ways and traditions are considered primitive.

They all listened intently to the old man.

'Would we have been rescued if they had stopped us leaving?' Liam asked.

'Hard to say,' Father Murphy, 'the rain forest is immense and not easily penetrated. Your guardian angels did a good job, I'd say.'

Then the women came over and spoke to Father Murphy; they led the nine to another long hut where there were the usual hammocks.

'Let you all get a good night's sleep now, my children. Tomorrow we must try and contact the nearest town and let people know where you are. Your parents must be very worried about you all, but rest assured, you are safe now and will soon be reunited with your folk.

They agreed whole heartedly and gratefully fell into the hammocks, to sleep a long undisturbed sleep.

16

Celebrating rain

When the nine awoke, they were surprised to find rain pouring down, the heaviest rain they had ever seen. Going to the hut entrance they were startled to see the darkness caused by the rain. Where was the sun gone?

They stood wondering when it would stop. After some time, a young girl came running to their hut. She carried a wooden plank with fruit of different kinds on it.

She smiled at the nine and said shyly 'Hell-o, I am Puri. PaPa M'fee come soon to speak with you.'

'What about this rain? We have not seen rain since we started walking, is it unusual?' Liam was interested in this strange country. Hot and humid one moment and pouring with rain the next. They had no raincoats or umbrellas; how would they travel in this weather?

Puri the young girl, smiled and nodded. 'Yes, the rains have come on time, it's very good.'

She looked delighted and Hughie and Alfie looked at each other, their eyebrows raised.

'You like the rain?'

'We need the rain and then our crops grow; no rain is no food, no rice.' She spread her hands and shrugged her shoulders. 'Rain means we are happy now, tonight we will dance and have much singing.'

'Where we live, we don't like the rain much; we certainly don't dance when it rains,' explained Alfie.

'We get too much rain where we live, in Ireland; if we had to dance and sing, we would never have time to anything else.' Hughie grinned around at them all.

'A lot of rain in your country? No, our rain comes for a short time only and then disappears for one year.'

Nonie considered all this, 'well that's not so bad then, you can plan parties and picnics without having to cancel them.' She beamed around at the others.

'When will Father – I mean PaPa M'fee come to see us?' June was anxious to be gone, even though these were such friendly people.

'Soon, very soon. He go to find boat that moves without paddles, you know, a big boat?'

'Oh! A motorboat! That's great,' said Mira in relief. No more paddling for the cousins it seemed.

They relaxed a bit then and sitting on the grass mat on the floor they ate some fruit. Puri sat with them and did not seem to be in any hurry to leave.

'Tell us about yourself Puri, you go to school, don't you?' Bella was interested in learning about the people here, now that she knew they were not in danger of being married to any strange men.

'Yes, I go to Mission school with all the other children here and PaPa M'fee come often to see how we progress. He is good man, and he looks after many schools like ours and clinics which help the sick people in the villages.'

'Are there many villages around here?' Rose asked, wondering how far they were to a town with proper communication.

'Lots of villages like ours, some nearer, some far, far away. PaPa M'fee must go to all, a lot of work and boat travel.'

'You can only reach the villages by boat?' Faith did not like the sound of this at all.

Liam hated having to question Puri so much, but he decided to plough in anyway.

He started asking all the things they needed to know. Where were they? Where was the nearest town? Did the village have telephones or mobile phones? Was a boat the only means of transport?

The girl listened quietly and answered the questions in her best English. She welcomed the chance to speak to these strange young people.

There were lots of villages like hers, all along the banks of the river. The town was a long distance away and it was only in the town that there were telephones and even televisions! She was very proud to relate all this and was somewhat puzzled when she saw the dismay in the faces of her listeners.

'No television?' asked Alfie with his mouth open and his eyes as big as saucers.

'No mobile phones?' chorused the girls, thinking how awful life must be here for the young people.

'How do you get in touch with your friends?' June felt sorry for Puri.

'When we go to the villages for visits or special feasts and parties, then I see my friends and other family members,' she explained, smiling. 'Sometimes I write letters to my friends in far-off villages.'

'Letters?' The nine looked at each other. In their world no one wrote letters, except for the younger ones to Santa at Christmas.

'What if you needed to see somebody really urgently, what would you do?' Faith could not understand this life at all.

Puri's face brightened up. 'Ahh! If my mother or father ill? No problem! We send a boat for the nurse or doctor, or maybe sick person can travel on boat to clinic. No problem, see?' She beamed around at them all.

This was not of course what they had meant. What about just chatting away to their friends, every free minute of the day?

'Is your school here, in the village Puri?'

They had not been able to explore this place as it was late when they arrived and now it was lashing rain.

'Yes, it is, not a big, big school. When I am older, I go to a bigger school in Lampang and study there with my friends.'

'Oh, a boarding school. You will have to sleep there as well?' Mira and Rose were fascinated to hear about her life.

'Where is Lampang, is it a town?' Liam asked hopefully.

'Very big, big town,' confirmed Puri, spreading her hands wide.

'So, is that the nearest town to here?' Liam was trying to work out where they were exactly.

'Yes, many, many people live there, many stores and lots of things to do. I want to live there when I leave school, maybe.'

The rain continued to pour down and the morning was spent questioning poor Puri, who did not seem to mind. The cousins felt that they would not be travelling much today, by the looks of it. They did not mind too much as they were just beginning to lose the soreness in their legs and arms from all the walking and paddling.

After midday the sun suddenly appeared, and the heat was immediately evident. The puddles outside the huts were dry in a short time, much to the disappointment of the younger children and Alfie and Hughie who had a great time jumping in them and getting muddied all over. They had lost interest in hearing about Puri's life earlier and had quietly left the hut without anyone noticing.

At mid-afternoon there was great noise and excitement as a group of people arrived and caused a stir among the locals.

In their midst, was Father Murphy. He greeted them all, smiling broadly.

The nine were relieved to see him. Now they could be on their way again.

Father Murphy came up to where they were siting in the sunshine. 'And how are the survivors, this day? Did you sleep well and has everyone been looking after you alright?'

They agreed everything was fine and told them that Puri had been very good at explaining where they were.

'Are we leaving now Father?' asked Liam hopefully.

'Ah well, there is a slight problem. The man who owns the boat says there is something wrong with the engine and it needs to be looked at by a mechanic nearby. But it should be all fixed by tomorrow and then we can be off.' He looked around happily at the nine and noticed the disappointed faces.

'Don't be worried, I have sent a letter by boat to the chief of the next village who will get it sent on to the town with the boat which brings the post.'

It all sounded so primitive to them. How easy their life was with the internet and mobile phones. They could not imagine the lives of these people without these things.

'I have also enquired about the plane crash and hopefully some news will be waiting for me there in the village, where our church is.'

They sighed sadly. Another day without knowing where Alva and Joey were and how their parents were coping without them.

Bella as usual, was the most practical. 'Look, there is no point being disappointed. There is nothing we can do about the delay. Another day or two won't make too much difference.'

They knew this was true and decided to make the most of the extra day of rest.

That night in the village there was an air of excitement. The women and young girls seemed to be busy all that afternoon and now with night upon them, all the fires were blazing, and torches attached to poles so that the whole area was bathed in a rosy glow.

Everyone entered the biggest long hut, and it soon became apparent that a party was ready to start.

The long wooden tables were laden with fruit and there were big calabashes standing on the floor beside the tables. The rain had now resumed, and it was bucketing down outside.

The nine were seated at a table along with lots of young children and Puri sat with them too. The air of celebration was contagious, and the cousins were starting to enjoy their time here. Father Murphy was present also and sat at a table with the older people.

Everyone piled into the food which was brought to their table and passed around on big banana leaves. When they had all eaten, they leaned back, totally satisfied.

'That's the first meat we have eaten in ages,' murmured Bella. 'Yummy!'

'I loved those chicken wings,' nodded Alfie, wiping his mouth with his hand.

'Me too,' agreed Nonie and Hughie, holding their bellies.

They all agreed it was the best chicken they had eaten for months.

Puri shook her head smiling, 'no, not chicken, we only eat that when they are old and don't lay eggs anymore. Chicken too expensive to eat.'

'Really? What meat was it?' Everyone was surprised.

'Those be the legs of frogs. Do you know these creatures?'

The nine looked at her in disbelief.

'Frogs?' Alfie and Hughie looked like they might be sick.

Bella reassured them by telling them that the French people ate frog's legs, and they were considered a delicacy.

'We'll all be hopping around the place, wait and see,' said Faith mournfully.

'As long as we don't start croaking,' said June sweetly. She liked the food and was not complaining.

When all the food had been cleared away, tables were pushed back to the walls and there was suddenly music. The party had begun!

The youngsters were looking at the various instruments being played; they were different to any they had ever seen. There were long pieces of wood fitted with two strings and played with a bow; lots of drums which were wooden and beaten with hands, boat-shaped instruments like a xylophone and played with two hammer-type drum sticks and some bells which were played by the children and made a high-pitched chime which sent shivers down the backs of the nine. The music was exciting and not at all like music at home.

During a break in the performances, Father Murphy appeared with a guitar, and everyone clapped the elderly man.

He launched into some old Irish songs and seemed to be enjoying himself thoroughly.

The listening locals were very polite and smiled and nodded along with the old priest.

Some of the cousins had heard the songs before but did not know the words at all.

Then after more refreshments were passed around, everyone looked at the newcomers and beckoned them.

Father Murphy shouted over to them, 'you are expected to entertain us now, it's your turn.'

The nine looked horrified. 'I can't sing,' muttered Alfie and nudged his brother. 'You can; you know that hymn they sing at school, you sing it.'

Hughie was a bit embarrassed, but egged on by Nonie and the others, who certainly did not want to do anything, he bravely stood up and began his hymn.

'When creation was begun……'

When he was finished everyone clapped loudly and Father Murphy beamed at him, he had started to accompany Hughie on his guitar and that gave the youngster a lot of confidence and he sang loudly and clearly. At the chorus, everyone had joined in with him.

Liam clapped him on the back, 'well done Hughie, you were great.'

Then Nonie was told to get up and sing, which she did shyly. She gave her best performance of 'This Old Man', and everybody clapped the table and added their part to the catchy song.

Then it appeared there were no more singers from the group after Nonie sat down.

'Ah can nobody do an Irish dance at all?' Father Murphy was disappointed.

Faith and Rose nudged Mira and she accepted her fate and got to her feet.

It was no problem for her; she was a champion dancer and accompanied by Father Murphy who suddenly produced a tin whistle from his pocket, she entertained these generous people who were entranced by her dancing and high kicks.

After she sat down, lots of the younger children got up and tried to copy what they had seen. There were legs kicking all over the place; some kicked too high and landed on their bums, amid roars of laughter.

It was very late when the party eventually ended, and Father Murphy gave everyone a blessing and said good night.

17

Another river trip

The motorboat chugged down the river and it was a lot faster than paddling a canoe. The nine leaned back and felt relaxed and happy to be on the move again.

The jungle on either side would disappear at times and the river would widen to a very broad river, when they could not see the banks, then it would divide and narrow again, and the jungle would reappear.

Hours passed and then they pulled into a village as the rain began to fall again. The villagers all greeted PaPa M'fee and welcomed his passengers too. They had lunch in the usual long hut and today it was rice and fish again.

The rain passed after an hour and the sun was out again. The people did not want Father Murphy to leave, it was obvious. He explained in their language why he must go, pointing to the nine and they understood and looked sympathetic.

On they travelled, and Hughie, Alfie and Nonie napped. The light was going when they suddenly became aware of lights and sounds that had been missing for what seemed like a long time. Buildings were visible with electric light, and vehicles, and people on mopeds. They had reached the town!

They all leaned forward excitedly and started chatting noisily. Father Murphy smiled at them and said, 'here we are then, back to the madness of towns.'

They landed and Father Murphy hailed a taxi near the pier which was a busy place with lots of boats and canoes.

'We are going to meet the Governor of the district first and tell him all about your accident and he is well connected and hopefully, will have some news about the plane crash. You'll then have a nice comfortable room at the local convent, which is also the community centre. You can all have a nice hot shower; would you like that?'

'Would we what?' laughed the nine.

Oh, the thoughts of a hot shower with soap and shampoo brought them all to near hysterics!

The Governor was a gentle man, in fact, all the villagers except the first ones at the first village, were all the same; gentle, polite and kind people.

He listened silently as Liam explained what exactly had happened to them.

He understood and nodded. He complimented on their travels so far and told them that they were brave people.

'Everyone in Chiang Mai has heard about this plane crash, it was a terrible thing. There are some survivors, but nobody knows that you were among them.'

The nine listened in silence as he relayed all this. Only some survivors, that meant that not everyone had survived, didn't it? What about Alva and Joey? Would the Governor know?

Finally, Bella asked him if he knew the names of the survivors?

The Governor shook his head sadly. Father Murphy now took control.

'Right, we must take all your names and relay them to the Consulate in Chiang Mai, we must get word out to the television stations and local media that you are all safe and sound and try and track your relatives.'

All their details were written down by the Governor, watched over by Father Murphy. They would now be sent electronically to the Irish Consulate and that should start things moving fast.

They were all pleased and left the Governor's office in a state of high excitement.

The convent campus was thirty minutes away and was a large complex; there was the convent, a school and clinic, a community hall and a special area where elderly and infirm people lived in care facilities.

The sisters welcomed them all and looked a bit taken aback by the ragged clothing and disheveled state of the nine.

They were led into a long hall and boxes of clothing were produced and the nine encouraged to help themselves.

'Oh, this is great! I can't wait to get out of these horrible smelly clothes at last,' gushed June and all agreed with her.

Liam found a pair of shorts that were almost new and fitted perfectly. There were boxes of t-shirts and Hughie, and Alfie were grabbing them and fighting over them.

'Stop fighting lads, you only need one, we will be home soon.' Liam was grinning at them; he could not stop smiling. The awful adventure was nearly at an end.

The girls rummaged among the boxes and found something to suit everyone. They all went for shorts and long-sleeved t-shirts; the weather was too hot for anything heavy.

There was a box of new underwear too and they all eagerly grabbed what they wanted.

When they were finished, one of the sisters came and led them to a dormitory in the school building and they were shown where the showers were located.

'When you are all ready, please come down to the dining room and we will have dinner ready for you,' she told them.

'Oh, boy, quick, let's go,' said June.

There followed thirty minutes of pure pleasure as the nine washed the jungle out of their hair and minds and luxuriated in the hot water, soap and shampoo. They all resolved silently that they would never take this luxury for granted, ever again!

The nine young people that entered the dining room looked a lot different to the ones who had been in the Governor's office. They felt different as well. They felt much more human and alive.

This time, the meal was really chicken, no doubt about it and the nine ate their fill eagerly. It was followed by mangoes and guavas.

June asked the sister in charge if she could possibly see a nurse at the clinic as she was getting low on insulin. She was assured that she would be the first to be seen the following morning at the daily clinic.

Father Murphy came and bade the nine good night. He was staying with the local parish priest of the area and would return in the morning.

He noticed their new attire and told them they looked very smart and that their parents would have no trouble recognising them. They laughed at this and felt very uplifted.

'You are all in for a big surprise tomorrow morning; I won't spoil it by telling you what it is though, you would not sleep well tonight if I did, and you sure need your sleep.'

They looked at him, puzzled but he only smiled and put his finger to his nose. 'Sleep well,' he said and then he was off.

The school was unoccupied at this time as it was the holiday season, so they had the whole dormitory to themselves.

They sat considering their situation and feeling relieved and contented, even though they knew there were some survivors and did not know if Alva and Joey were there, they could only feel hopeful and optimistic, they did not dare to think otherwise.

Hughie and Alfie did not ask any questions as they were unaware of the information received at the Governor's office.

They went outside the boarding school and wandered around the campus. It was all well-kept, and they waved at the elderly people sitting outside their little houses further down. The entrance was nearby, and the gates were locked. There seemed to be a park across the street. It was busy here, with lots of traffic and car horns hooting. They continued their walk around the compound and soon found a small gate which was open. Liam and Bella led them safely across the street and they entered the park. There was lots of grassy areas which seemed strange after the jungle; there was a lake with ducks swimming on it. All around, there were people strolling and children running and playing.

The nine wandered around watching everything and amazed to see all these people behaving normally.

'It's almost like being home, isn't it?' Rose remarked.

'Except it would not be this warm in the evening,' commented Mira.

'Wish we had a football,' said Hughie.

'I miss our dog,' moaned Alfie.

Bella laughed, 'we don't have anything to wish for, we will soon be on the way home. I can't wait to get to Perth again, I'll never fight with my mom again.'

They all agreed that life would be different now and that they would never forget what it was like being separated from all the familiar things.

They found themselves outside the park later There were many cafés and eating places and lots of people sitting outside talking. They strolled past and wished they had some money for a fizzy drink.

They passed a big open-air restaurant and could see a television on a huge screen. They passed by and soon became aware of people pointing to them and talking to each other.

'What are they pointing at?' Nonie wanted to know as she stared back at the people.

'Maybe there is news about us on television,' suggested Faith.

'We're probably famous already,' said June, lifting her shoulders and walking straighter with a bit of a swagger.

'Just look at her, she thinks she's a film star!' Rose rolled her eyes and nudged Mira.

The girls looked around them. They were certainly getting a bit of attention they knew, especially from a group of men on the corner of the street. They did not really like the look of them.

'We should return to the school, I think,' said Bella who also did not like the attention they were getting.

'Nobody knows where we are, we never asked if we could leave. I bet we could be in trouble with the sisters,' Liam was anxious too and it was very dark by now. 'Come on lads, fast march.'

They crossed the busy street again and headed for the safety of the school.

The elderly people they had seen earlier were now missing. They probably all inside their huts and asleep, they guessed.

Once inside the building, they headed straight up the stairs to the dormitory. The small convent building was in darkness, and they guessed the sisters were all in bed.

They were excited by the change in their lives and looked forward to what came next. They each picked the bed of their choice and were delighted to find the toothbrushes and toothpaste which were left on the lockers by the thoughtful sisters.

'Good night, everybody,' shouted Hughie and ran from the bathroom and jumped into his bed, followed by his happy brother.

18

Nine in real trouble

The nine slept soundly. The hot shower, good food and the stroll around the park had worn them out physically and it was such a luxury to sleep in a lovely soft, comfortable bed again. The hours crept by, and the moon flooded their dormitory without their being aware of it. All nine faces had a most peaceful and happy look on them.

Their lovely sleep was shattered suddenly about three o'clock in the morning. They were rudely shaken and told to get up fast. Sitting up in the dark they thought there was a mistake and that they were dreaming. But no, at each bed, there was a figure in black, pulling the covers from them and grabbing their arms, forcing them from the beds.

The younger boys started to cry and immediately their mouths were covered by hands, and they were bundled from their beds.

Liam and the girls tried to ask what on earth was happening. The men spoke in their own language, and it seemed that only one spoke some English, as he kept saying, 'hurry, please hurry.'

Rose objected and said that Father Murphy would be here soon and was bringing them to Chiang Mai and that he would be very angry if they were not there.

'Ah, yes, PaPa M'fee, he say come now, quick, double quick.'

This information stunned them. Did Father Murphy say that and had he sent these men for them? It all seemed wrong somehow.

'Remember what Father Murphy said about a big surprise this morning? Perhaps this is it.' Faith whispered, as she put on her sandals.

Bella was very annoyed, 'Surprise? I think it's a most awful bloody shock.' She scowled at the figures who were pointing to the door of the dormitory.

They were silently marched down the stairs and on towards the back of the building and led to a back door and into a waiting van, the doors of which were wide open for the nine tousle-haired cousins.

Then the van took off with the nine and three big men with the children.

The van was driven at speed and the nine were flung about inside it. Nothing was said to them until a short while later; the van stopped abruptly and a voice shouted 'Out, out.'

They were roughly herded into a large empty warehouse-type building and pushed into a storeroom at the back. They could see a crude toilet at one end. There was no furniture or anything here, just a dusty floor and a single light bulb burning in the middle of the room.

'What is going on and why are we here?' demanded Liam.

The biggest man turned to a younger man; indeed, he was only a boy, maybe in his late teens.

'You must not worry, you go soon, when money come, you are free, don't worry please.'

Bella spluttered in indignation, 'you mean you have kidnapped us, you horrible people?'

The young man who spoke quite gently, urged her not to be angry.

'Angry no good, please stay quiet and it will go well.' He seemed desperate for them to comply with the leader.

June then came forward; she was not afraid of these thugs. 'Listen here, my medicine is running out and I need to see a nurse or doctor. I am a diabetic.' She stood her ground, arms folded across her chest, her chin out.

The older man asked something, and the young man shrugged and replied in his own language.

The older one now pulled the young man out, muttering angrily all the time. They heard a key being turned in the lock. They were prisoners in a windowless room and were in shock.

How had this happened? Where was Father Murphy?

Alfie and Hughie were crying and then Nonie started. June stamped her foot in anger and the others just looked at each other, helplessly.

They were locked in. They each went and tried the door; it was a big metal door and was firmly shut, there was no way they could open it.

'Right lads let's sit down and consider our position,' instructed Liam.

They all sank to the floor despondent and worried. They had been kidnapped and what would poor Father Murphy do when he called for them at the convent?

'I don't think we have been taken very far from the convent. We were only in that van for about ten minutes, wouldn't you think?' Liam turned to look at the girls.

They all agreed that it had been a short drive with lots of turnings of corners, it could be an industrial area, they thought.

The younger children were all quiet now and listened anxiously to the older one's discussions and opinions.

'We must stay calm whatever happens,' Bella advised. 'Father Murphy and the Irish Consulate will know what to do.'

That thought brought them some comfort. They continued to sit and think silently. They had no idea what time it was, if daylight had come. If only there was a window to look out!

'If we hear any sounds of people about, we can scream and shout, can't we?' Faith looked hopefully around. 'They won't want us making noise, will they?'

'Would they bring us to a place where ordinary people might be working? I think not,' said Mira and big tears rolled down her cheeks.

'To think that we were so near to being rescued; it's just not fair,' snorted Bella.

Time passed and they spent some time playing games to amuse and distract the young boys; Nonie sang a few songs, then gradually they grew silent.

They all sprang up alert and eager when the door was opened. Three men entered carrying food and water. Again, it was the young man who spoke to them gently.

'Eat now, drink water. Things not so bad here, eh?' he asked them, smiling.

He did not get any smiles in return. The nine glared at him with angry faces.

'Where is Father Murphy?' asked Bella.

The young man seemed embarrassed and turned to the other men and spoke in his own language. They laughed loudly as if he had told them a joke.

'Soon, soon he will come,' murmured the young man, looking down and avoiding their eyes.

Then they were gone, and the children looked at the food. They had no appetite now, they drank some water and sat down again. There was nothing to do but wait.

It was much later that June began to feel unwell. She got up and ate some of the food on the tray, then sat down again. 'I feel awful.'

'You didn't bring your backpack,' Rose said.

'I didn't have time to think, did I?' June lay down and closed her eyes.

Now Rose was worried and looked at Liam.

'We have never been in a situation like this before and it could become serious, if she is low or too high.'

'What can we do?' asked Bella.

'That young fellow understands English, we must make him understand that June needs medical help.' Liam told them.

'Yes, I'd say that he has been to school and is quite intelligent, also he is the most human of them all.' Mira admitted.

'He doesn't shout like the others either,' said Faith.

'What do you think, June? Can you hold out for a while longer do you think?'

There was no answer, June was asleep.

This scared the older ones half to death. What if she went into a diabetic coma? What would happen? They were suddenly terrified as their hopeless position became clear.

Time passed slowly, they woke June several times and tried to keep her talking but she kept falling asleep.

The door opened again and the young man and the big bully, as they thought of him, entered. The food tray was taken, and more water was left.

This was their last chance; it might be night again and they might not return until morning.

Liam and Bella got up and approached the young man. 'Please listen, my sister is a diabetic, she needs medicine, please take her to a hospital, now. If she goes into a coma she may die.'

The young man listened intently. He then relayed the information to the bully, who laughed and waved Liam away as though he were a fly.

Bella put up her hand, 'please listen.' She went over to the sleeping June and pulled up her sleeve and showed the men the monitor she had on her upper arm and then the pump she wore around her waist.

Again, the bully laughed and pointed at June, shaking his head. The young man looked at what Bella was showing them, and he did not laugh. His face looked concerned and serious. He spoke again to the bully, who just took him by the arm and led him out the door. They heard the key again being turned in the lock.

The eight stood in silence and looked at one another.

'What will happen now, will an ambulance come for June?' asked Alfie who did not really understand at all.

'Maybe they will bring a doctor here to see her,' said Hughie, nodding his head. 'That would be good.'

The others said nothing. They did not think that June's condition would make any difference to these criminals.

Liam sank to the floor, his head in his hands.

19

Safe again.

How strange time seems, when there is no daylight. Nobody could have even guessed the time, or how long they had been imprisoned; it was just endless.

'They are all looking for us, we mustn't worry,' Bella kept reiterating this.

They knew this must be true, but where were the search parties?

They kept trying to wake June but by now, she was groggy and seemed to think they were still in the jungle.

'Get me some of those guavas and some nuts, will you?' She looked all around her. 'I can hear a waterfall, will we swim?' Then she fell asleep again.

This was worrying and had never happened before. At home her diabetes was well managed and June herself very aware of everything about her condition and was even able to educate her friends about it.

'I can't hear any waterfall, can you Hughie?' Alfie looked around at his brother.

'There isn't a waterfall, it's just June, she's a bit dunleerious, I think.' He looked at Bella for confirmation.

'Delirious, Hughie,' Liam said and couldn't help laughing, despite his concern. 'Dun Laoire is a place near Dublin. We went there for Dad's fiftieth birthday.'

That distracted them for a while and Rose and the other Barber children told their cousins about the great time they had and the exciting part about jumping into the sea at the Forty Foot, as it is called.

The day or night, dragged on and they were getting more and more distraught. There were no sounds to give them any hope. This was obviously a disused place and could be miles from anywhere.

They must have all fallen asleep as they were suddenly startled out of their stupor or sleep by sounds from outside. Thumps and thuds came and then there were five cousins pounding on the metal door and screaming loudly. They only had their hands to bang on the door, there was nothing else they could use.

Voices could now be heard and something metal banged the door which did not budge. They heard shouting then and a huge noise, like a machine of some sort.

They stood back and watched as the metal door began to sag in the middle and then the door was forced open. There were people in uniform outside. They appeared to be army people.

Then Father Murphy appeared and rushed to the children, behind him two people with a stretcher. Liam pointed to where June lay sleeping and they quickly put her on the stretcher and left the place at a trot to a waiting ambulance. Father Murphy ushered them all out and the soldiers stood and made way for them. Some of the sisters were there too and soon the eight cousins were whisked off in a bus.

They were brought again to the convent and a hot meal was ready for them. Father Murphy was with them the whole time. He appeared pale but was calm and spoke softly to them, reassuring them that June would have excellent care and they could go and see her at the hospital later.

They felt better after a hot shower. The police were in the dining hall when they came down again with Father Murphy.

They wanted to talk with the children and find out about their experience which they were only too willing to do. Their relief was so great that they could only smile at each other, when they knew that June was alright.

'How did you know where to find us, Father Murphy?' Liam asked this question for them all. They could not believe that the priest had known where to look.

'It was the young boy who you told about June and her diabetes. He was once a pupil of the mission school in one of the villages until he came to the town and got involved with these bad men.

They are part of a drugs gang here; there is a huge problem with drugs and organised crime in this part of the world and unfortunately it is a very profitable business, so young Marku got involved. However, he realised that June was in danger, and he had heard about diabetes and his conscience would not allow him to keep silent, even though it could cost him his life.'

'So he went to the police?' Bella asked.

'No, he came straight to me first and told me. He knew that I would know what to do. The police might not have believed him as he has come to their notice before.' Father Murphy sighed and shook his head. 'So many young men like Marku get caught up with the gangs, it's too terrible.'

The police heard the story of their abduction and seemed satisfied. Now they were all anxious to see June.

Father Murphy brought them to the local hospital in the bus that the sisters had, and they trooped in to see the patient.

They found her sitting up in bed, being fussed over by two nuns, a nursing sister and a doctor. She looked as if she were enjoying every moment of it and did not seem any the worse for her experience.

'There you are, I thought you were lost!' She turned to her attendants, 'these are my sisters, brother and cousins.'

Later back in the convent it was again nighttime. The sisters were worried about the effect the abduction might have had on them, especially the younger ones. They need not have worried. They were in good spirits and were surrounded by treats of all kinds, sweets, chocolates, fizzy drinks. June was considered fit enough to leave hospital so there were all together again.

Father Murphy was there and said that tonight he would be staying the night here at the convent.

'It seems you can't be trusted to stay inside and not go gallivanting about, where people saw you and knew who you were after seeing your photos on television!' He said this with a twinkle in his eye. 'It appears that all the television stations were showing photographs of the survivors from the crash. Famous, you are!'

'Yes, I suppose we should not have gone outside, we just thought it was alright.' Bella now knew that they should not have gone.

'What about that surprise Father Murphy?' Nonie looked expectantly at him. 'We thought first that the men coming and making us get up was the big surprise, but it wasn't, was it?'

The old man laughed so much at this that tears ran down his face. 'That was a surprise? More like a horror movie, it was. Maybe I should not have told you that, me and my big mouth.'

Nonie and the boys were disappointed.

'Is there no surprise?' Hughie asked, his face full of sadness.

'Of course there is! But now we must wait until morning, and you must get a good night's sleep with no wandering about in the middle of the night.'

They were too willing to agree with that and retired soon after. In the darkened dormitory the older ones talked about their experience. How long had they been imprisoned? They had forgotten to ask that question. It didn't matter now though; they were safe again.

The older ones all silently wondered about the young man Marku; would he get into trouble with the gang and would the gang now be caught and locked up. As they dropped off to sleep, they knew *that* was a question they must ask Father. They would forever be grateful to Marku, he had quite literally, saved their lives.

20

The big surprise

There was a crowd in the entrance hall when the nine descended the stairs for breakfast the next morning. The young people were startled to see cameras flashing and the sisters were having trouble keeping the throng away from the nine.

Father Murphy was there too and told the photographers that they could take one picture of the nine but that was all. He gathered them all together and they all posed for the cameras, looking at the crowd of people in amazement.

Now the sisters and Father Murphy requested everyone to leave as the children must have their breakfast before departing.

Microphones were thrust in the priest's face and questions were being fired at him non-stop. He smiled patiently and put his hands up. Speaking quickly in the local dialect he subdued them, and they slowly drifted away, apparently content with his answers.

The nine were starving again after their long sleep. They were soon eating a huge breakfast of eggs and bacon which they could hardly believe. Bacon! There was toast and fruit too.

Father Murphy looked at his watch and left the room, only to return two minutes later. He looked excited and his friendly face was flushed.

'Time for the big surprise now my friends. If you are all finished, we must go. Say goodbye to the sisters, as I doubt you will be seeing them again.'

The nine rose from their seats and shook hands with the sisters, thanking them for their hospitality and said they hoped they might see them again sometime.

They once again all put on the well-worn backpacks and were led out the back door into the sister's garden which was a large compound and then stood still, not believing what they saw. There was a helicopter on the lawn!

The three youngest were jumping up and down with excitement.

'Are we really going in the helicopter?' Hughie and Alfie hugged each other in delight.

Father Murphy hurried them all onto the aircraft, explaining that the Irish Consulate had sent it. It would be the quickest way to get to Chiang Mai; otherwise, it would take days paddling and trekking through more jungle.

How relieved they were to hear that. Then they were rising above the town and then the jungle, not quite believing that their adventure was coming to an end.

It took over an hour to reach their destination and they now knew why Father Murphy wanted them to leave early.

By the time they landed, the rain was torrenting down again and visibility was nil. A bus was waiting and very slowly, the ten passengers were taken away.

Because the visibility was so poor, the journey seemed never ending to them all.

On the way to the Consulate, Liam asked Father Murphy about the gang. Had the police caught them and was Marku safe?

'He is in a safe place, never fear, folks. He did his Christian duty and now the police know exactly how many and who the individuals are. They were rounding them all up as you slept last night.'

They were relieved to hear that Marku was safe. He deserved to be, after being brave enough to contact Father Murphy, knowing that the gang would never forgive him for his betrayal of them.

The big gates of the Consulate swung open as they approached, and now they were in front of a big modern building. It seemed strange to see something so new and modern after their time in the jungle and villages.

Father Murphy helped them all down and led the way to the big door, which opened as they neared it.

Alfie and Hughie screamed when they saw who was waiting for them, smiling broadly and crying at the same time, Alva and Joey.

It was an emotional reunion with everyone crying and laughing and asking questions all together.

Then it was time for Father Murphy to leave them. The helicopter was waiting.

They all shook hands, then hugged and thanked the kind man. They knew that they owed their lives to him and the contacts he had.

Now it was time to sit and talk non-stop for hours and just gaze at the other two survivors and hear their story. Tomorrow was another day and would bring them all back to Perth to recover a bit before heading back to Ireland.

They had questions too to be answered.

'Where did the rest of the plane come down, Alva?' Bella was curious as to why they never found any wreckage.

Well, the story was simple; the rest of the plane was quite close to where they were. The tail had twisted like they had suspected and was pointing in the opposite direction.

All the passengers had survived, they now learned with relief, with only some minor injuries. However, because of the inaccessibility of the area, help took days to find them and release them from the wreckage as half the plane was on broken trees, not on the ground. Then they had sent parties off to search for the tail section. When they found it eventually and no bodies, they guessed that the children had all survived and were somewhere in the jungle. They were searching in the wrong area just as the children were, walking in the wrong direction.

They absorbed all this information in silence.

'So, you were not terribly worried about all of us being lost?' Nonie asked this, remembering how worried they had all been.

Joey laughed, 'not terribly worried? We were worried sick at the idea of you walking in the jungle and wild animals and all sorts of dangers.'

'We thought you would all starve to death or be eaten by a wild animal; I didn't sleep a wink.' Alva wiped her eyes at the memories of the past few days.

They all nodded solemnly. Yes, a lot of awful things could have happened to them, yet here they were, all safe and sound.

'Do you all want to stay here for a while, and we could explore that nature reserve and see wild animals in their natural habitat?' Alva asked them all, when they were all feeling more normal again.

'It might help you all forget the awful time you have had, walking in the jungle.' Joey looked at them all, smiling.

Alfie spoke for them all. 'Are you JOKING Mum? We've seen LOTS of animals in the REAL wild, and it was SCARY; the jungle is just TOO scary. I just want to go home.'

For once, nobody disagreed with him.

Printed in Great Britain
by Amazon